HIS ONLY BEGOTTEN SON

A Gangster Father
Missing from his Son's Life

The Son
An Future NBA Prospect

A Mysterious Murder
A Prison Sentence

V. PHILLIPS

Published by:

SureShot Books Publishing LLC

P.O. Box 924

Nyack, New York 10960

www.sureshotbooks.com

Table of Contents

Guilt can be a good thing. It's the soul's call to action. The indication that something is wrong. The only way to rid your heart of it is to correct your mistakes and keep going until amends are made.

-   **FATHER LANTOM**

The Interrogation?

DeAndre didn't notice how much Tabitha had bled on him until he pulled his lanky arms into the short sleeves of his t-shirt to ward off the chill of the interrogation room. The sight of her life smeared in dark splotches across his belly and jeans made hot tears pool in his eyes. He did not know that a person could bleed so much. He had never wanted to know that.

"How did this happen?" He whispered to the empty room.

He would have cried if the arctic blast of the air conditioner hadn't dried his tears before they had a chance to fall.

Still, he held them back, knowing that he would have plenty of time for crying when this was over. If it was ever over. He tried not to give the resolution a timetable, but his mind kept screaming, "one year… two years… it'll never be over."

The frigid air penetrated his pores. His teeth chattered as he looked around the hollow space. The interrogation room was no more than a cube with three plastic chairs spread out around a worn wooden table. A previous occupant had carved "stop snitching" into the table's surface. The walls were covered from floor to ceiling with knobby egg grates to soundproof the room. DeAndre imagined a young black kid sitting in one of those chairs while two white detectives beat him. It seemed like a plausible occurrence, even beneath the watchful eye of the security camera wedged into the apex of two walls.

DeAndre knew that people were watching him at that moment. They were analyzing how he stood, walked, and reacted to being left alone in an empty room for so long. He did not want to act predictably, but what was the body language of an innocent man? Was it that much different from a guilty man's? He did not know, but he was sure that whoever was watching him did.

He hoped the footage of him in the room didn't end up on TMZ the next day. The local news would run the story. He could deal with that. But TMZ is a national entity that had a reputation for ruining celebrity lives. He didn't consider himself a celebrity, not yet. If TMZ ran this story, he never would be.

Those wandering thoughts made the room seem colder. DeAndre hugged himself as he stood and paced. "Where are these detectives? We need to get this over with. "He slid his long brown arms through the sleeves of his t-shirt and rubbed his palms together.

"What is taking them so long?"

He made furious laps around the room. They had taken his phone, and there was no clock. It had to be nine a.m. If it was nine, then he had been awake for twenty-seven hours straight. That was a long time with no sleep. Especially after the night he had. To be honest, he was in no position to talk to the cops, but that fact didn't stop him from wishing that they would hurry.

He ended up leaning against one wall. Hazy images washed over the interrogation room.

The first thing he remembered was the roar of the crowd. Then the floor trembling with stomping feet as they chanted his name.

His name.

No one else.

He'd spun in a slow circle with his long arms splayed like an eagle's wings as confetti rained from the roof of the arena and clung to his sweat-soaked limbs. He'd felt like a gladiator claiming glory after a fresh victory, no, not a gladiator Caesar. A King greeting loyal subjects after a hard-fought battle.

The people converged upon him, pressed together so tightly that they had no choice other than to move and sway as one mass. Reporters fought their way to him, shouting questions that he barely heard over the chaos. Microphones were shoved to his lips. Somehow, he gave the answers they wanted. He spoke of his past, present, and his bright future, blazing like a NorthStar within an ocean of black for all to see and follow.

The night had been his alone. Everyone wanted a picture of, or to talk to, DeAndre Harris. For at that moment he was more than a man. He was a god.

And then... darkness.

The applause sounded less like clapping hands and more like gunshots booming in his ears. The converging mass of congratulatory fans became the horrified shouts of stampeding partygoers sprinting to safety in all directions. DeAndre ran too... until he saw her sprawled on the floor with blood pooling around her still body. The triumph of his night seemed a million miles away then, like a distant date x'ed off his calendar years gone past. His heart thundered as he knelt and cradled her bloody head in his lap.

"Somebody call 911!" He shouted. "Please! She's dying!"

Camera flashbulbs become flashing police lights.

DeAndre blinked away the memory as the interrogation room door swung open. He was leaning against a wall as two white men entered. Both wore khakis and faded Polo shirts with bronze badges sewn over their hearts. One had shaggy red hair. The other a blond buzz cut.

Carrot Top carried a tablet. "Have a seat, Mr. Harris, "he said.

DeAndre didn't move. He watched them sit through suspicious eyes. Carrot Top gestured to the only empty chair. Only then did DeAndre sit.

"Don't say a thing." DeAndre thought. There was no way that he could go down for this. He wouldn't be the reason Michael went down either. He wasn't a snitch.

Besides, this whole thing was an accident, a misunderstanding. Nobody should be in trouble for that.

He'd been caught shoplifting once when he was about eleven. He and his mom had been living in a black suburb outside of Chicago. His friend Delbert had stolen a package of beef jerky. DeAndre had taken nothing. The store security officer waited until they had left the store before giving chase. Delbert ran the farthest. DeAndre watched the soles of Delbert's feet kicking hard as he was slammed to the concrete with a knee in his neck to pin him down. DeAndre had been interrogated then, to by the security officer and the store's manager. He hadn't committed a crime, so they couldn't arrest him for anything. Delbert had done the stealing, not him.

They called his mom. She entered the manager's office with her lips and posture tense. She cocked one eyebrow and threw DeAndre a glare that said the earth would shake beneath his feet if he didn't tell them who had stolen what and caused all this trouble. Soon after... he ratted on Delbert.

DeAndre was slowed to go home with his mom. There was a cop car parked outside Delbert's house. Delbert was being led out of his house in handcuffs by the time DeAndre was getting out of his mom's car. The look of betrayal Delbert gave him was enough for DeAndre to swear that he would never snitch on a friend again, regardless of the consequences he faced. That... and no other kids would talk to him as long as he lived in that neighborhood. He didn't make friends again until they move to Raleigh, North Carolina the next summer.

The cops slumped in their chairs. Nothing unusual. Just another day.

Carrot Top asked, "How are you?"

DeAndre shrugged. "I've been better."

Carrot Top nodded. "Great game last night. You won me two-fifty. Covered the paint spread and everything. The miracle three-pointer that won the gave let me tell you it was phenomenal." When DeAndre didn't respond, he asked, "Want water? Bag of chips? There's a machine down the hall."

DeAndre looked to the blond cop, then back to Carrot Top. "I'm good."

Blondie sat up and rested his elbows on the table. "Look, kid. We're not here to play with you. We know who you are. Trust me. There's a parade of press vans lined up and down Salisbury Street, waiting to see if you'll walk out of here free or in handcuffs. Me? I couldn't care less. You're just another stain that I have to clean up. Who you were before tonight is a whisper of what you will become if you don't cooperate with us? "Somebody is going to prison for a long time. The only person who can make sure that inmate isn't DeAndre Harris is you." "He sat back and crossed his arms with an exclamation of finality.

DeAndre's heart was in a boxing ring going rounds with his ribcage. He kept seeing his mother's face, her eyebrow cocked, her expression telling him, "You'd better tell them something."

Despite the chill, a hot trickle of sweat rolled down the nape of his neck. "I don't know anything," he told them.

Blondie snorted. "You're going to lie to me like that? The NCAA Championship was held at the BBC Center. Afterwards you went to a Kappa Alpha Phi frat party on Brent Road. I've got five eyewitnesses standing right outside that door who know exactly what I'm talking about. We found a pistol. A Beretta nine-millimeter. Three people put that gun in your hand. Two of them can ID you as the shooter."

DeAndre's fists clenched in his lap. "They don't know me."

Carrot Top winced. "Who doesn't know DeAndre Harris?" Blondie cut him off. "Yeah, you make the cover of last month Sports Illustrated. You're on Sports Center every hour on the hour. There isn't a soul in this country that couldn't pick you out of a crowd. There's a runt in a China shop dribbling a basketball and wearing your Jersey as we speak. "He leaned over and whispered; you can't run from this kid." "People know you. "make

DeAndre ran a shaky palm over his face. "Did it ever occur to you they could be lying?"

"I've got a news flash for you," Blondie said. "Everybody lies in this game. The winners tell the believable lies first. The losers go to jail for life."

DeAndre held his gaze, then turned away. He took a long breath and let it out before burying his face in his hands, thinking: 'Twelve hours ago I was living the best moment of my life. Now I'm facing the worst.'

"Mister Harris," Carrot Top said, scooting his chair closer to the table. "We're not here too, we're not your enemies. A young woman is lying dead in the morgue, and it's our job to find out what happened. We know that she was your girlfriend. If you cared anything about her, you would help us. That's all we're asking for. Help in closing this case."

DeAndre faced him, his jaw clinching. "You think I killed Tabitha?"

"We don't know. We follow the leads you're giving. As of now, all fingers point to you, no one else."

DeAndre buried his face in his hands again, then stood up with a growl. He banged his fists against the wall. "I can't believe this is happening to me."

Blondie tapped the table. "We get it. You've got a stellar life ahead of you. Believe me, we know you don't belong here. A lot of young black guys like you sit in that seat like it's a throne and talking to us about a murder is the one moment they know was destined to happen to them. They may as well have been born in a jail cell. From the cradle to the cage, you know you're not like them."

"My attorney and go home."

Blondie chuckled. "Home? You're not going home." He stood. Carrot Top followed his lead. "You're being charged with first-degree murder. That's a capital offense punishable by death. There is no bond, so you can't bail out. The only phone you'll be using is in the county jail."

The words 'first-degree murder' echoed in DeAndre's ears. "Murder? You can't charge me with murder. I didn't shoot her. I didn't even have a gun."

Both detectives walked to the door. Carrot Top opened it and left. Before Blondie had a chance to exit it, he turned to DeAndre with a smirk. "You lawyer'd up. Now you'll have to tell it to the jury. See if they give a damn, because I don't." He stepped into the Hall, then thought better of it and turned back. "You know, it's too bad that you won't make it to the NBA draft. Vegas had you going first. Two-to-one odds. The best in history. Now you're going to prison."

DeAndre had a feeling that the sheriff's deputy was coming for him. He'd been waiting in the holding cell for at least two hours. It was a long wait, but he didn't mind. this was the only time, in his short career, that he was in no hurry to leave the jail.

Alone, he still wore his Armani suit and Stacy Adams shoes. The thought of having to take them off made him sick to his stomach, yet he stood as the deputy approached.

The guy was at least 6'3, a formidable height. Three inches shorter than DeAndre. What the cop lacked in height, he made up for in girth. He had boulder sized shoulders that were almost twice as wide as DeAndre's, and that set the width for the rest of his hulking mass.

His name tag read Samson.

Samson stopped at DeAndre's cell, then examined some papers in his hand. DeAndre stepped closer just as Samson was opening the door with a set of huge brass keys.

"You ready, Harris?" Samson asked, his voice rumbling like an avalanche.

"I guess."

Samson held up a jingling set of handcuffs and a longer set of leg shackles. Their glam sent kaleidoscopic shards of light dancing around the sale. "turn around, it won't take but a minute."

DeAndre wondered why he had to wear shackles, like some kind of slave. He wasn't going to run. He had been out of jail on a million-dollar bond for the six months it took the state to complete his trial. The judge wouldn't give him a bond at first, but his mom hired an attorney whose son had been a college roommate of the governors. After that miracle, his mom still had to put up her house and $10,000 cash. A high price to pay for a few months of freedom.

If he wanted to run, he would have done it then when the option was open. The thought had crossed his mind. He could have made it to the Honduras or further before they knew that he was gone; any place tropical where the women were bronze, and the currency exchange worked in an Americans favor. He stayed because he didn't want his mom to lose her house. Of course, she could buy another one, but he never once thought that he was going to be convicted at the trial.

Still, he put his palm's flat against the wall and spread his legs.

Twenty minutes later he was twisted sideways in the cramped back seat of Samson's squad car taking his last ride through downtown Raleigh.

Samson switched on the radio. A commercial.

DeAndre looked out the window as his home whizzed by in a blur. It was spring. Not a cloud in the sky. Women wore short skirts and tank-top blouses is as they strutted to work in sneakers.

The radio buzzed with a newsbreak. "Onetime NBA hopeful, DeAndre Harris, was convicted of 1st degree murder and sentenced to life without parole in a Wake County court room this morning. Twenty-two-year old Harris was the leading NCAA scorer who first made headlines by opting out of entering the NBA draft following his freshman season, to remain in college and earn a bachelor's degree. He played four seasons for NC State and lead his team to three consecutive national championships. Harris was convicted of killing Tabitha Murray, his live-in girlfriend, while the two attended a fraternity party are Brent Road in Raleigh.

"NBA legend, Curly White, had this to say…"

Another voice commandeered the airwaves. "I hate to see a talented young man throw his life away and in such a disrespectful manner. It's bad enough that we've got these these young hoodlums killing each other for nothing; police killing black men for nothing. But now, one of our best has gone and thrown his life in the trash pile. For what? Most people don't have half the opportunities that young man had. Now he'll die in a prison instead of being a positive role model for our troubled youth."

DeAndre noticed Sampson's eyes on him in the rearview mirror.

The reporter came back on. "Many in the NBA echoed White's sentiment and sent condolences to Tabitha Murray's family."

Sampson reached down and turned off the radio.

DeAndre was thankful for the silence.

***

Central Prison was only a few miles from the Wake County Jail. The hulking monstrosity sat squat amidst manicured lawns and small businesses neighboring it on Western Boulevard. Built in the eighteen hundred, Central was the only institution to house death-row prisoners and the death chamber that killed them. DeAndre had once mistaken it for a college as he drove past one day, until a friend riding with him pointed out the razor-wired fences. After that, he drove past it at least once a week and never thought that he would enter its bowels as a condemned man.

Deputy Samsung pulled into the prison and checked his firearm at a guard station. Then they drove around back to an enclosed garage where Samson entered and waited until the garage door shut before getting out of the car.

DeAndre shuffled inside, wincing with the bite of the leg shackles cinched tight around his ankles. They paused at a closed sliding door. Beside it was a control booth with tinted windows and a female correctional officer inside. She pushed a button on a digital control panel and the door slid open.

Samsung led DeAndre to a holding cell and told him to sit on a concrete bench that ran from one end of the cell to the other. The officer in the control booth pushed the button, and the door slid closed. DeAndre remained standing.

The concrete bench looked as if it had once been painted a solid grey. Now it was concrete, with chips of grey paint scattered across brown and yellow stains. He wouldn't sit. He stood looking out of a Plexiglas window as Samson walked to a tall wooden desk and handed a prison guard a stack of papers.

Sampson leaned over the desk on his elbows. The other guy doubled over with laughter. They kept that up for a few minutes. A little later another guard walked near. Samson and his friend leaned in close to whisper in hushed tones, then both glanced toward the holding cell at DeAndre. The guard nodded, then began processing DeAndre's paperwork as Samson walked back to DeAndre.

The cell door opened. Sampson stepped in, and removed DeAndre's shackles, then left.

The cell door closed.

DeAndre just sat and sat for a very long time.

A fresh prison guard arrived three hours later whose name-patch read Smith. He was a short, and stocky white guy with spiky blonde hair and green eyes. He carried an empty cardboard box. "I'm going to strip search you," he said. Smith tossed the box at DeAndre's feet. "When I'm done, you put your street clothes in there. Later I'll give you a marker to write your home address on the box."

DeAndre nodded. "What am I going to wear?"

Smith stepped into the cell and dropped a bundle of ratty looking clothes on the bench beside DeAndre. "You're wearing an offenders' uniform."

He made DeAndre strip naked in the holding cell. Satisfied that DeAndre wasn't concealing anything, he walked out. The door closed behind him.

The Brown pants DeAndre was given fit in the waist but were five inches too short. The tail of his dull gray t-shirt wouldn't reach his belt line, so he couldn't tuck it in. One dingy sock was longer than the other. Both were brownish and nappy. White low-top sneakers of the nineteen-seventies, All-Star type were the only new garments he was given, and they weren't much. He laced them up and took a few steps. The rubber soles were so thin that he might as well have been wearing nothing at all.

He hadn't had the pleasure of shopping for sneakers in years. Boxes of them arrived at his apartment doorstep as if a stork had dropped them off. He wondered how the various companies knew his size. Agents called him offering foreign cars, exotic women, and asking if his mother needed a new house. They gave him stacks of cash, and of course, free sneakers whatever shoes he wanted. All he had to do was ask.

DeAndre look down at the shoes on his feet, if he could call them that, and he knew that his days of luxury were over.

He folded his suit and stuffed it in the box along with his other clothes. Discarding those items felt like he was dropping white roses into a casket as he kissed his life of freedom goodbye. Ashes to Ashes. Dust to dust. The gleaming image of success he'd once known was now a figure of rust.

A commotion was going on outside his holding cell. Three guards escorted a stocky black prisoner. The guy was older with salt and pepper hair. He wore the Brown pants that DeAndre wore, but also leather boots with thick black souls. He walked stiffly with his hands cuffed behind his back. The man's face was scratched, his lips gnarled as he cursed at the officers. DeAndre could only hear muffled voices behind his closed cell door, but he heard enough to know that the man wasn't happy.

They pushed the guy into a cell across from DeAndre and then removed his handcuffs before locking him inside. Instead of sitting, the guy paced around the cell like a tiger in his cage.

Officer Smith arrived at his cell a little while later with another guard in tow, a tall brown-skinned female. She wore her hair in thick braids piled atop her head.

Smith brought a black marker, as promised. He watched DeAndre scribble his mother's address on top of the box. He told DeAndre to leave the box on the concrete bench, then he led DeAndre out of the cell into an office.

Smith told the female, "Fingerprint him the way I taught you, then take a picture of his ID. Let me know when you're finished so that we can take him to the housing unit."

The woman nodded. Smith left the two of them together. DeAndre watched as she grabbed a pair of latex gloves and struggled to put them on. Up close, he assumed that she was at least five-ten. She had almond-shaped eyes and a sharp nose. Plump lips hovered over a dimpled chin. DeAndre wondered what such a beautiful woman was doing working in a prison. A woman like her belonged on the cover of a fashion magazine.

She was finally able to get her gloves on and walked him to a tall machine with a computer console on one side and a glass tabletop on the other.

She punched keys on the keyboard, frowned, tried it again, then muttered, "I can't remember what I was supposed to type." she stood there thinking. She tried typing another set of keys. This time she sighed with relief as the machine hummed to life. She walked back to DeAndre. She took his left thumb and rolled it over the glass tabletop and smiled when an image of DeAndre's thumbprint appeared on the computer monitor.

"You don't have a name tag," DeAndre said. His voice sounded strange. He couldn't remember speaking a single word. The woman turned from him. He wasn't used to the subservient role that he imagined prison forced a man to play when it came to women employees. The way that she cut her eyes showed she was not accustomed to being in charge.

"What's your name?" He asked her.

"Melody," she blurted without looking up from her work.

"Officer...Melody?"

She wheeled around with the realization of her mistake. "M-A-R-T-I-N." My name is Officer Martin.

The day's events gave DeAndre no reason to laugh, yet the chuckle rose from the depths of his belly and pushed past his pain. Nothing could have held it back. Not even the grief of knowing that he was going to die in prison.

Martin peered out of the open doorway to make sure no one was spying on them. She whispered, "please don't tell anyone what I said, period, we're not supposed to tell you our first names."

"What can I do with your name?"

"I don't know," she confessed. "they told us all kinds of stuff at orientation." She sighed. "it's my first day in prison too, and I hate it already."

He didn't ask why she hated her job or any other questions. Her laughter died away, and she continued to fingerprint him.

"I used to be a software programmer, but the company I work for went bankrupt," she said while stealing glances at him, trying to make it seem as if she wasn't looking. "I worked there for four years. After the company closed, this was the only job that I could find. They're paying me one fifth of what I made last year." She gritted her teeth. "I've been a prison guard for all of six hours, and I'm ready to quit. They tell us not to talk to the guys. They say that you're no more than animals in cages, but you seem normal to me. You deserve to be treated like a human being."

DeAndre's mouth opened to speak but said nothing. What could he say? He'd heard lots of stories about prison, but he had no idea about the horrors awaiting him. He was sure that every other officer wasn't as nice as Martin, and the prisoners may be brutal. Because he had no idea what to expect, he couldn't comfort her.

He said, "maybe it's not that bad. Give it some time."

Just then, A man screamed from somewhere outside the office door. "I'm telling you that I wasn't transferred to Scotland Correctional!" I ain't going!"

DeAndre saw that it was the same black guy that they had brought in earlier period he stood in the middle of the open room with three white property bags resting at his feet.

Four officers appeared from a side door. All men.

"Look, Stewart, I don't make the decisions around here. I just follow orders. Maybe you can get it straightened out when you get to where you're going, but you're not going to yell at me."

Stewart balled his fists. "You hard of hearing? I told you. I'm not going anywhere. Take me back to the hole. I don't care."

The other officers watched Smith from a distance, waiting to see what he would do. One of them eased his hand to a can of pepper spray in a holster on his belt.

Smith yanked out his own can of pepper spray. "Stewart, I'm giving you a direct order to submit to restraints and prepare for transfer to another facility. Are you disobeying my direct order?"

Stewart Watched Smith's hands, then met his eyes. ", care anything about your direct order. I haven't done anything to you, but if you spray me with that Mace, I will take that can an shove it down your throat sideways. I ain't playing around."

Smith hesitated and look to the other officers, unsure of what to do. One of them nodded just once to let him know Smith Bray and fired a hissing stream straight into Stewart's eyes.

Stewart ducked and dodged most of the maze, rushed in and scooped Smith by his legs, slamming him to the ground. "didn't I tell you not to mace me?" Smith's body moved like a monkey until he was sitting face up.

The other officers stood and watched, waiting to see if Smith would get the upper hand. They only sprang into action when it was clear that Smith couldn't defend himself. They yanked Stewart off as he thrashed and struck out at them as the two secured his arms, while the third bunched his ankles together to secure his kicking legs.

Smith climbed to his wobbly feet. It took a second for him to regain his composure. When he did, his red eyes looked at Stewart. Smith slide a retractable blade from his utility belt and jerked it open with a swipe. Stewart wriggled in the officers' grasp, unable to get free. His wild eyes focused on Smith. "what are you going to do? Hit me? You need all of these men to help you?"

Smith ran at him, slashing Stewart in the face. A gash opened across Stewart's forehead and a River of blood bubbled out, but Stewart didn't yell or utter a word of protest. He stared up at Smith, face grimacing. Infuriated by Stewarts silence, Smith kept hitting him, so hard that the officers could barely keep Stewart steady.

"Hold him still, Smith."

Instead they dropped him to the floor where he lay there unmoving. The four guards drew their legs back and started stomping him. They kicked him anywhere their boots could connect.

Inside the office, Officer Melody Martin whispered, "Oh my God."

DeAndre watched her tremble. He knew that he wasn't supposed to do it, but he took her by the hand and lead her deeper inside the office, away from the door. He asked, "you're supposed to take my picture, right?"

She didn't resist, but she kept trying to look at the mail. "what?"

DeAndre led her to a station where a chair rested against a white backdrop and a camera stood on a tripod in front of it. "My picture," he said. "you forgot to take my picture."

Martin's face was a mask of confusion. "Are you kidding me? They're killing him out there."

All went silent out in the open area. He no longer heard the dull thuds of boots on slash. One of the officers yelled, "yo, he ain't breathing!"

"What?" another responded. "resuscitate him!"

Sounds of an officer giving Stewart CPR echoed into the office. DeAndre thought about how strange it was that a second ago they were trying to kill him, but now they were trying to save his life.

"I'm not getting locked up for this," one of them said.

Tears streamed down Martin's cheeks. "I've got to go out there. This isn't right.

DeAndre grabbed her wrist to pull her back. "You don't want to be here? Me neither. None of that matters now." he sat her down in a chair. "You can't change anything going on out there."

Martin sat there debating. Her hands trembled at her sides. DeAndre reached out and wiped her tears. "I'm going to sit down right here while you take my picture." He sat in the chair in front of the camera.

Martin looked at the camera. "I don't remember how to do this."

"Try," he said.

Martin looked at him for a long time. Soon her breathing slowed. Her hands stop shaking. She took the picture.

Outside of the office, Stewart inhaled a deep breath of life.

TWO

Tabitha was a squiggly wet mass in his grip. DeAndre tried to embrace her, to keep her close to him, but the harder he grasped her, the easier she slipped away from him.

Then she was off, slaloming through the back-alley streets of Tijuana past frolicking college students who were happy, drunk, high off drugs, or high offspring break in a foreign country.

DeAndre kept up with her as best he could. She held out her hand for him to grab, but he only succeeded in brushing her fingertips every so often. Then a converging mass of people would cut him off and he had to push his way through to catch up again.

She always waited for him. Smiling. Standing there just long enough for him to get close, then she would take off again.

He ran and caught her once. She kissed him in front of a small bridge with children gathered around a man selling shaved ice with flavored syrup from his cart.

Tabitha laughed against his lips and pushed away, like it was a game. But DeAndre wasn't laughing. He didn't understand why she kept leaving him. He needed her. For three years they'd been inseparable. His 'away games' were the only time they were apart, and even then, it killed him to be far from her. Their bond went far beyond companionship or love. DeAndre depended on her presence like a kidney, a lung, a breathing heart some internal organ whose absence would surely kill him.

He reached for Tabitha again. This time her limbs were slick with a gooey substance, almost like the yellow and red syrups the ice shaver squirted into his frozen treats. The goo helped her slip away, no matter how hard he tried to stop her.

"Tabitha!" He cried out.

And then they weren't on the dilapidated Mexican side streets any longer. They were at the frat house on Brent Road. The place was empty except for him and her. A rap song of money, sex and murder boomed through the speakers though the DJ booth was empty.

Tabitha wasn't trying to escape him now. He sat cross-legged on the hardwood floor, cradling her leading head in his lap. DeAndre swiped blood-matted hair out of her eyes, and she blinked while staring up at him, lips gasping for air like a goldfish out of water as if she had forgotten how to breathe.

"Stay with me, baby, "he chanted. "Stay with me…"

Yet he saw her slipping away again. No matter how hard he tried to hold on.

DeAndre jerked upright in his bunk. His breath sputtered in ragged jerks, like an engine choking on its own fumes. Sweat dribbled from his forehead. The dark cage was lit by a dull blue nightlight, gleaming like a midnight moon against the dull steel surfaces of a short steel table bolted to the wall, a steel toilet and sink welded together, and rectangular locker bolted to the concrete wall.

He wondered if he'd been better off trapped in his nightmare.

De Andre got up and stooped to look out of the square window punched through his steel cell door. The outer cell block was quiet and dark. His view afforded him no glimpse of a clock. He assumed that it was sometime around three in the morning. He walked back to his bunk no more than a steel slab with a plastic mattress on top and laid down. He took a few deep breaths, then closed his eyes with Tabitha's face fresh in his mind.

It took a moment to drift off, but sleep did come.

Someone was banging on his door ten minutes later, yelling, "Get up! Get up!"

DeAndre opened his eyes. It was murderously bright in his cell with the lights on. He squinted at the black face scowling at him through the little square window.

"Count time!" The officer yelled.

"Okay," DeAndre said back, but the guard didn't leave.

"Count time!" He hollered again.

DeAndre rolled over and pulled the cover up past his head. He didn't know what else to do. Seconds later keys jingled in the cell door's lock. The door swung open and a squat officer charged into his room. He straddled DeAndre and wrapped his hands around his throat.

"Did you hear me say count time?"

DeAndre clutched at the cop's wrists but was afraid to do more. He'd never faced this type of aggression. Common sense told him that the officer was a figure of authority. He wasn't supposed to fight officers. Yet he couldn't breathe. His eyes were bulging out of his head. He saw spittle coating the guard's lips from the exertion of his force.

"I know who you are!" The officer spat. "And I know what you did. Killed that pretty girl for nothing!" He squeezed DeAndre's throat harder. "Somebody outa kill you!"

DeAndre's eyes were rolling up in his head when he felt the great weight lifted from his torso and the strangling hands jerked from his throat. When his eyes could focus again, he saw an older black officer with salt and pepper hair shoving the younger against the far wall of DeAndre's cell.

DeAndre recoiled as far away as he could, clutching his throat, gasping for air. Maybe a second more and he would have been dead. As that thought crossed his mind, he wished the cop had killed him. It would have been better than traveling the perilous road now set before him. He had to die eventually. Why not get it over with so that he wouldn't have to suffer the ills of life in prison? Death seemed like such a merciful escape from the turmoil that had become his life.

"I wasn't going to kill him," the younger officer told the older one. "I wanted him to know the rules. Inmates have to stand up for count."

The older guy let him go. DeAndre read the older guy's nameplate. It said Leach. He looked at the younger cop who glared at DeAndre with eyes still full of rage, and DeAndre, cowering on his bunk. With a hand on his elbow, Leach ushered the other officer out of the cell. Then Leach stood there with his hands on his hips, belly bulging over his belt, eyes yellowed and ancient. "You alright?"

DeAndre nodded.

Leach scratched his chin. "Gibson's a good guy. He gets a hot head sometimes." DeAndre didn't say anything. "Next time stand at your door for count time. It's so we can make sure you're alive. That's the prison's policy."

DeAndre nodded again.

Leach took a step toward the door. Before leaving, he turned to DeAndre and said, "When somebody runs up on you like that, protect yourself. This may not be the world you're used to, but you must adapt to it. If somebody gets tough, you need to be tougher. It doesn't matter who it is, inmate of staff. Nobody respects a coward in here. Nobody."

DeAndre looked down to his feet, finding it hard to meet Leach's eyes. "I don't want any trouble."

Leach grunted. "Don't matter what you want. If you don't stop it, it'll only get out of control." Leach left and slammed the cell door behind him.

***

Only a few conversations ceased when DeAndre entered the chow hall. He fell into a long line of convicts waiting for their breakfast trays, wishing he was invisible.

He felt eyes burning a hole through his cheek, though his own eyes stayed forward. Their harsh whispers drifted to his ears. "There he goes right there." "He's taller than he looks on TV." "Look at that punk, killed that girl like that."

DeAndre grabbed a food tray from a slot in the wall. Spongy scrambled eggs. A shriveled-up piece of sausage. Soggy toast. No butter. No jam. Instead of making his belly growl, the sight made his stomach turn.

The other cons didn't stop staring when he cast his eyes out over the crowd looking for somewhere to sit. There were thirty or so tables, each with four stools welded to them. Whites sat with whites. Blacks with blacks. Hispanics with Hispanics. Everyone was color coded and age segregated into their neat little groups. Rarely did he see a black man sitting with white guys, or an older man sitting with a younger man. Everyone seemed to know their place.

Everyone except DeAndre.

He spotted an empty table in the back, near a yellow cooler where men were lined up for juice. He sat and nibbled at his eggs and toast. The sausage he didn't touch. He had avoided processed meat in the real world and didn't plan on eating it now.

"Yo, you gonna eat that turkey sausage?" Someone asked him.

DeAndre looked up as three men sat down with him. One black, one Mexican one white guy. All were young and around his age, but somehow less threating than the other convicts.

The Hispanic guy asked him again, "You gonna eat that meat?" DeAndre shook his head. The sausage disappeared from his tray in a flash. The guy took a huge bit and chomped with his mouth open. "I used to be like you," he told DeAndre. "I wouldn't eat this crap when I first got here. I kept waiting for them to serve something good, but something good never came, so I started eating it. It's not so bad if you can chew past the gristle."

The white guy scooped his eggs onto a slice of bread. "Quite lying, Chino." He looked at DeAndre. "He'll eat the balls off a wombat if you let him."

"That's not true," Chino protested, shoveling a spoonful of eggs into his mouth. "I'd eat everything but the balls." He turned to DeAndre. "Know how to make turkey sausage?" DeAndre shook his head. "See, they take a turkey and lead it into a dark shed with a trail of breadcrumbs. The turkey thinks there's a whole load of bread in there waiting for him. But when she stumbles inside, she sees a three hundred-pound porky the pig, grinning in the corner. They lock the turkey inside, and nine months later…" Chino holds up his half-eaten slice of meat. "Turkey sausage." He took another bite and smacked on it. "It happens."

The white guy slapped Chino on the back of his head. "Didn't your mother teach you any table manners? We don't talk about sex at breakfast. Only lunch."

Chino stopped chewing and stared at him. "Damn Sidewinder. You know I don't have a mother."

DeAndre thought that it must have been true because Sidewinder looked down into his plate and didn't say anything more.

If Chino was offended, it didn't last long. He looked to the other black guy at the table. "Danny, you gonna eat your eggs?" Danny slid his whole tray over to Chino. Chino scooped up the eggs with his spoon and fingers. "Danny don't talk much," Chino said. "But he's smart, and he's dangerous,"

Danny didn't say anything.

DeAndre glanced around and noticed that people were staring at him. He decided it was time to leave. He felt comfortable in the confines of his cell.

Just as he was about to stand, a group of black men approached their table and surrounded it. All the newcomers wore dreadlocks, some in later stages of growth, but dreadlocks just the same. All stood with their broad shoulders back and chests bowed out as a show of strength.

The one behind Chino clamped a hand on his shoulder. He leaned over, close to Chino's ear. His grimace showed a mouth full of diamond encrusted platinum teeth. "I told you to see me Monday. It's Tuesday."

Chino kept his wide eyes focused on his plate. "My money didn't come through yet, Kevon. My sister will send it soon. I'm gonna get you straight."

Kayvon stared at the side of Chino's face. "You better."

"Didn't I always? When have I ever been bad business?"

Kayvon squeezed Chino's shoulder hard enough to make him wince in pain. "Your first time will be the last." He let go and stood up. "I don't take shorts." Keyvon looked to DeAndre. "What are you looking at?"

"Uh nothing."

Kayvon laughed. "You're alright, bro. I know who you are. Nothing will happen to you. "He looked at the men seated at DeAndre's table and shook his head. "But you might want to watch the company you keep. Birds of a feather flock together. These dudes are lame. Are you?"

No one responded.

Kayvon and his crew stepped away. As soon as they were out of earshot, Sidewinder let out the breath he'd been holding in. "I hate that dude."

He glared at Chino. "I don't know why you deal with him. He's nuts."

Chino shrugged. "He sells the biggest stripes. Ain't nobody pumping slabs of Sub Oxone like his. Most hustlers are selling half of what he's giving for double the price. Why wouldn't I buy from him?"

"You weren't complaining when you were hunched over your toilet throwing up. What d'you say? 'I ain't never felt this good.'"

Sidewinder rolled his eyes.

DeAndre asked, "Who was that?"

Chino pushed his tray away. "Kayvon."

"Is he a gang leader or something?"

Chino looked to Sidewinder, his eyes asking if DeAndre could be trusted or not. Sidewinder shrugged, so Chino said, "He's not the leader. He's high up in one of those gang sets though. Which one, I don't know. They're all trying to kill each other. Either way, Keyvon only does what he's told to do."

DeAndre thought about that. Kayvon had him trembling. It was a feeling that he didn't like.

He got up and walked out alone. He had a feeling that he and Kayvon weren't done.

Getting accustomed to prison life was like dying and being born again into an alternate reality a twilight zone where the abnormal was normal.

Decades-old dust stained creases where the cinder block walls met the concrete floor, the ceiling...everywhere. When prisoners swept or mopped, they did no more than swirl the dirt around into the clouds that settled again or puddles of brown water. No place seemed safe to touch without the risk of contracting some type of disease.

Many of the men looked dirty too. They wore dingy clothes, unkempt beards, and their hair shaggy. They shuffled throughout the prison like walking dead. Some watched television from sun-up to sun-down simply because there was nothing else to do.

A few prisoners tried to talk to him, but soon realized that DeAndre didn't have much to say. The probing questions that they thought sounded friendly and harmless came off as prying and nosy. DeAndre ignored them and shrouded himself in an aura of silence. He didn't want to talk about his past life. He sure didn't care to talk about himself. And he sure as hell didn't want to talk about basketball.

A concrete cage became his best friend and sanctuary. For the first week or so he left it only for chow call. The prison outside of that six-by-eight concrete block had nothing to offer him. He didn't read. He didn't write. He laid in bed, staring at the walls, feeling like a cadaver in a coffin.

It only took eight days for him to realize that he was becoming one of the walking dead prisoners that he'd looked down on when he first arrived. His stubbled cheeks were sunken pale from lack of sunlight. The whites of his eyes were bloodshot. He couldn't stand to look at himself in the hazy cell mirror.

He forced himself to go outside for yard call.

Central Prison's recreation yard was a concrete dust bowl. Two-thirds of the towering barrier were facades of prison buildings. The biggest obstacle was a relic of herculean strength. The Wall. A thirty-foot-tall monstrosity that had been standing strong since the late 1800's. There was no grass. Just an example of concrete molded by two basketball courts running head-to-head. Old men played shuffleboard against the wall. Mexicans played handball against the wall at the far end of the yard. He saw no free-weights. Groups of men were doing push-ups, pull-ups, body squats, and strenuous calisthenics.

None of that was of interest to DeAndre.

A pickup game of half-court basketball drew his attention. Six black men were playing three-on-three and going at it. DeAndre recognized none of the refined techniques that he had learned from some of the best coaches in the country, but the men could handle the rock.

The best on the court was tall and dark-skinned with a bald head and long beard. He trotted up and down the court shirtless, pecks and biceps bulging beneath rippled and tight skin. Despite his physical appearance, signs of age were clear on his face. DeAndre guessed that he was in his thirties or forties. Way too old to be schooling the twenty-something on the court with him. He got the ball and wouldn't pass it. Just dribbled straight through his defenders and dunked for two points. The sparse spectators hooted and cheered. DeAndre was unimpressed.

"Think you could beat him?" A man behind DeAndre asked.

He turned and saw seven or eight black men sitting three benches up on a set of steel bleachers. DeAndre didn't remember seeing them when he first walked out. The only face that he recognized was the gangster, Keyvon, but even he, with his air of malice, wasn't the center of attention. The group sat in somewhat of a protective circle around one man—a slim brown-skinned guy with a brush cut and waves.

"Gator," Keyvon said. "That's the dude I was talking about, the guy in the center." Gator never took his eyes from DeAndre. He lounged on the bleachers, damn near laying down with his elbows propped behind him. "You heard what I said?"

DeAndre shrugged his eyebrows. "Were you talking to me?"

The group laughed. A few turned to look at Gator. When they saw that he wasn't laughing, they stopped laughing too.

Gator asked DeAndre, "Who else was I talking to?" His boys chuckled again. "Do you think you could beat him?"

DeAndre gazed at the men who were waiting for him to respond. Their scrutiny twisted knots in his belly. "Who?"

They laughed again. One of them said, "I think he's retarded. Gator."

Gator shook his head. "Nah. He ain't retarded." His eyes remained steady on DeAndre. "Did you get your degree?"

'Of course, he knows who I am,' DeAndre thought. A part of him didn't want to say anything. What did a college degree matter to these guys? He wanted to walk away, but these weren't the type of guys that he felt comfortable turning his back on. "They sent it to me through the mail."

It had been the most demoralizing moment of his life. First, he got a letter telling him that he wouldn't be allowed at the graduation. All that night he paced his apartment, thoughts of Tabitha and the shambles his life was in, prominent in his mind. He'd been robbed of the very thing that he had refused to enter the NBA Draft for, the act of crossing the stage.

Gator nodded along. "Damn shame. All the work you put in. For what? Them to turn their back on you. Nah. That ain't right."

DeAndre wasn't in the mood to talk about his past. He knew that it was a hot topic, yet it wasn't unavoidable. He started walking away.

"Don't do that, "Kayvon told him, standing with his fists clenched. "We ain't done talking."

DeAndre faced the group again.

Gator gave no indication that DeAndre's presence mattered in the least. His face remained an empty mask of indifference. "You never answered my question."

DeAndre glanced at the players on the court. The big guy had the ball, as usual. He backed down a defender, shoving him with his boulder of a shoulder to inch closer to the basket. When that wasn't enough, he shoulder-slammed the guy. Knocking him on his back, then dunked the ball and swung from the rim like an ape on a tree limb.

DeAndre looked back to Gator. "He's nothing special."

"Good. Because you're about to play him."

DeAndre shook his head. "I just came out here to get some air. I didn't come out her to play ball."

Gator flashed a half-smile as if DeAndre didn't get it. "I don't care what you came out here for."

No laughter followed his comment. The comment laced with an underlying threat.

He glanced to the big guy on the court, then back to Gator. I can't ball." He pointed down. "Look at my shoes."

One of Gator's team pressed a fist to his lips and snickered. "yo, look at him, still rockin' the state kicks. He'll break his ankles in them."

Gator's eyes never left DeAndre's. "Paco"

A slim light-skinned guy sitting beneath Gator looked up at him. "What up?"

"What size shoe you wear?" Gator asked him.

"Your size," Paco joked, slapping the knee of the guy next to him.

Gator turned his gaze to him. No laughter lived in his eyes.

Paco's smile faded. "I wear a thirteen."

Gator raised his chin toward DeAndre. "What size you wear, Schoolboy?"

"Twelve-and-a-half."

"Paco, "Gator said. "Give Schoolboy your shoes."

Paco looked down at his feet encased in crisp white New Balance mid-tops. "Gator' I bought these shoes with my last forty dollars. I had to wait four months to get them. If I give 'em up I can't afford any more for six months.

Gator didn't reply. He looked down at Paco. Instead of protesting further, Paco leaned over and began unlacing his sneakers. DeAndre watched him.

Paco glared up at him, eyes wet, lips snarling. "What are you waiting for?"

Gator told DeAndre, "Don't worry about Paco. Just switch shoes. He'll be alright."

The silent eyes of the gathered crowd told him that he had no choice. He sat on the bottom bleacher and took off his shoes. Once the exchange was complete, DeAndre stood and squatted a bit, testing the bounce of the sneaker. They weren't the best, but they would do.

***

Two men sat in a shaded corner of the yard, hunched over a chess board. Both were in their mid-forties, graying and short of temper. One wore a black knit Kufi, the other was bald.

The Muslin looked across the board at the bald man. "Preach. You ain't trying to move. I ain't got all damn day."

Preach wasn't looking at the board. His eyes were focused on the scene playing out by the bleachers.

"Preach!"

Preach jerked toward his opponent. "He shouldn't be talking to Gator and those guys, Percy. They're nothing but trouble."

Percy huffed then looked over to the men on the bleacher. "That's the Harris boy? The one played ball for state?"

Preach nodded.

"He shouldn't have done what he did. Killed that girl like that. Back in the day they would have had him bent over in a shower stall for that. I didn't feel no sympathy for him. A hard head makes a soft ass, so if Gator and his boys set him up to get tuned up, well, that's on him."

Preach pursed his lips. "You shouldn't judge people like that. "He looked over at DeAndre stretching, "You don't even know him."

"Neither do you, which is why I'm wondering why you care so much."

"I don't. I'm just..."

"Ya ain't never cared for none of these other young things running around here. We sat here together last week and watched two of them hack each other to shreds with shanks, and you didn't let out a hoot nor a holler."

French slumped in his chair. "You wouldn't understand."

Percy nodded. "You right. I wouldn't understand and don't give a damn. Move a piece."

Preach glanced at the board. They were about halfway finished with the game. "I ain't feeling it anymore."

"The hell you ain't. Percy pulled a wrinkled sheet of paper from his pocked and squinted at the hash marks scribbled on it. "You're up four-hundred-seventy-six games to four-o-two. I got this game in the bag, and that'll put me one closer to catching up."

Preach rolled his eyes. "You won't ever catch me."

"I'm closer than a blue-tick hound sniffing out your mama's funky behind."

"Don't be talking about my mama, Percy. Geraldine was a fine woman. Taught me how to do everything."

"Mm-hm. She should have taught you how to take this whipping instead of talking your way out of it. I'll talk about your mama, your daddy, and your cockeyed step daddy too if it'll get you to move a piece. I told you that I don't have all day. I have to wax the unit manager's office tonight, and I'd like to get started before I'm too old to swing a mop."

Preach frowned at Percy, then he sat up and readied himself to move. "Remember that you brought this punishment on yourself. I tried to give you a chance."

"Just move a piece, negro."

Preach studied the board then moved his queen. "Checkmate." He sat back.

Percy's eyes almost popped out of his head. "Ain't no way." His frantic eyes jerked all over the board until he saw it. The game was done. He started setting up the board for a new game. "Run it back."

Preach shook his head. "Un-uh. You had to wax a floor. Now you want to play again."

"That floor can wait 'til I get my revenge."

Preach looked out across the yard while Percy was occupied. The kid that Preach knew as DeAndre Harris was standing at the edge of the court staring at a pickup game, waiting for his turn to play. Preach wished that he could go over there and tell him that Gator and his gang meant him no good. But some lessons had to be learned the hard way.

***

Gator looked to the basketball court. The black bully had the ball. "Bull! Yo, Bull."

The big guy held the ball and looked to Gator. "Let me holler at you!" Gator yelled.

Bull thought about it, then sauntered over with his shoulders rolling and his black skin gleaming with sweat. He stared up at Gator, his chest bouncing. "What do you want?" He stared at the others with his lip curled in disgust. "Blue doesn't bow to red."

"I'm not asking you to bow, Gator explained. "This ain't beef, it's love. I've got some money for you. You like money, don't you?"

Bull looked to DeAndre then back to Gator. "You're talking, but you ain't saying anything."

Gator pointed at DeAndre. "I've have ten bricks that says Schoolboy her will mash you one-on-one. Five-point game."

Bull eyed DeAndre. "Ain't no way. I seen him on TV. You ain't hustling me."

"You don't get it," Gator said. "I'll make it fair. We'll spot you three points. All you have to do is make two shots. Who can't do that?"

Bull chuckled. "Two shots for ten bricks? You ain't for real."

Gator waved him off. "Put ten bricks on it and find out how real I am."

Bull looked at DeAndre again, sizing him up. He bounced the ball to DeAndre. "You get first rock."

Kevon cupped his hands to his mouth and shouted, "Ball in!" For all to hear.

Bull strutted out to half court and waited.

DeAndre turned to Gator. "Why did you bet on me?"

Gator cocked one eyebrow. "You said he wasn't anything special. Show me."

"What happens if I lose?"

Gator stretched back on the bleachers. "You don't lose. Everybody knows that."

DeAndre's knees knocked as he trotted out to Bull, looking like Goliath awaiting David. Bull's jaw clenched tight like the veins running a road map across the continent of his massive upper body.

DeAndre checked the ball to him. "What are the rules?"

Bull bounced it back. He swiped the ball out of DeAndre's hands as soon as he caught it. DeAndre watched him dribble up the court and dunk it. He brought the ball back and jammed it into DeAndre's stomach. "Ain't no rules."

The bleachers erupted in protest.

"C'mon, Schoolboy!" Gator hollered. "Don't lose like that!"

Of all the shouting voices, Gators was the only one that mattered.

Bull stooped into a defensive position. "This is going to be easier than I thought."

DeAndre's hands rolled over the worn leather ball. It had been an eternity since he held one. Over a year. But the feeling was still the same. There was energy in that ball energy that he had channeled repeatedly to conquer his fears and limitations.

He checked the ball to Bull. Bull punched it back. DeAndre dribbled with his left and stepped that way. When Bull followed, DeAndre slipped him with a behind-the-back crossover to the right and ran around him with ease. Bull tripped over his own feet trying to keep up and laid on his back, watching DeAndre toss in and easy lay-up.

Gator applauded. "That's what I'm talking about. Secure that bag!"

DeAndre ran back to half court just as Bull was dusting himself off. "Your ball," he said, tossing the ball to him.

Bull checked the ball to DeAndre. "You think you slick, don't you?" DeAndre tossed it back. "Not as slick as..."

DeAndre slapped the ball out of his hands and hurried up the court. He dunked with two hands then ran back and left the ball bouncing in front of Bull.

Bull snatched the ball and checked it to DeAndre. "What are you trying to do? Embarrass..."

DeAndre swatted the ball away again. This time when he dunked, he twisted in a three-sixty spin and hung on the rim after he'd jammed it down.

Gator's cheering group drew a new crowd of onlookers.

DeAndre ran to Bull and dropped the ball. "Three, four."

Bull checked the ball then held it as far away from DeAndre as he could. "I see that I can't play with you no more. It's time to end this."

DeAndre crouched in his defensive guard. His legs were loose. His arms elastic. The prison around him disappeared. He saw only Bull's eyes and heard the bouncing of the ball beating the pavement with the same rhythm of his heart. Bull jammed his elbow into DeAndre's solar plexus as he tried to back him down. DeAndre stayed firm and never gave an inch. With one final push, Bull spun and jarred his elbow into DeAndre's chin to send him back a few feet. Just enough to get around him.

DeAndre saw a blur as Bull dribbled past him. His legs pumped to catch up. Bull leapt for a lay-up and released it. DeAndre hoped behind him just in time to snatch the ball out of the air. He was down and jumping again to dunk before Bull knew what had happened.

When Bull realized how he'd been bested, he pushed DeAndre. "That's over the back!"

DeAndre back-pedaled to half court. "You said there were no rules." He tossed the ball to Bull. "Four up. Game Point."

At half-court Bull checked the ball and took off as soon as he got it back. DeAndre stayed in front of him, keeping his hips low and his arms wide. Bull tried to muscle his way round. DeAndre was there absorbing the blows. Bull faked left, then went right. DeAndre stole the ball and launched an arching jump shot so perfect that it sailed through the hoop and net without a swoosh.

"Game time," he said.

Gator was on his feet pounding his palms together. DeAndre peered around. The whole yard was applauding.

"That's right!" Gator shouted. "Game time! Go get my bag!"

Bull frowned at all the applauding people. He gave no warning before he charged. The game had DeAndre so loose that he danced away from the charge. He failed to throw up his hands and ate a right hook that made him see stars.

***

Preach hopped up so fast that he knocked over the chess board and scattered the pieces over the concreate ground.

"Man, what the hell is wrong with you?" Percy complained.

"He punched that boy, Percy"

Preach started toward the fight with his brow creased and his jaw tight.

Percy stood and blocked his path. "Mind your business, Preach."

Preach tried to step around him. "He ain't built like them, Percy. They'll eat him alive."

"Sure will," Percy agreed." And each of them has a piece of steel longer than your forearm and sharper than your razor slid up his sleeve right now."

Preach paused, knowing that he couldn't win.

Percy patted his shoulder. "A man has to learn to fight his own battles."

Preach sat down.

***

Gator said, "Kevon," and the man leapt off the bleachers between Bull and DeAndre.

Bull retreated but kept his fists high. "Kevon, this ain't got nothing to do with you."

Keyvon didn't say anything in response. He threw up his hands and advanced on Bull. Keyvon shot a jab that popped Bull in his chin. He didn't let up. He punched his fist into Bull's face until the big man tripped over the bottom bleacher and fell. Keyvon hopped on top of him.

A swarm of gray and black uniforms rushed past DeAndre as prison guards poured out of the building.

Kevon hammered Bull's face until two officers grabbed his arms and yanked him off. They slammed Kevon to the ground and wrenched his arms back to cuff him. Bull was too punch drunk to resist. He submitted to the cuffs with blood pouring from his nose.

As the officers were leading the two away, Gator yelled down to Bull. "Don't forget to pay me when you get out of the hole. I still want my bricks."

Adrenaline ran a race through DeAndre's veins. Everything happened so fast, and then it was done.

Gator stepped off the bleachers beside him. DeAndre noted that Gator was every bit as tall as him and looked in good health, albeit ten years older. He laid an arm across DeAndre's shoulders. "You did good today. Won me a lot of money."

"Yeah? What's ten bricks?"

"Ten packs of cigarettes."

DeAndre thought about it. "They don't allow smoking in prisons, and they didn't sell cigarettes."

Gator smiled. "As long as there is a gas station up the street and the state doesn't want to pay these guards a living wage, there'll always be cigarettes here. Forty dollars a pack. You won me four-hundred dollars."

"What about Bull? Will he pay after what Keyvon did to him?"

"He'll pay. And when he does, I'll break you off with half."

"What about Keyvon? He went to the hole for me."

"Nah, bro. He went to the hole for the cause." Gator started walking. He gestured for DeAndre to follow. "First thing you've got to learn about prison is to have no fear. Fear no man. No cop. No punishment. No consequence. Not even death. If you can learn to do that, this prison will fall at your knees and provide for you. Nothing will hold you back."

"Hold me back?" DeAndre asked. "Hold me back from what?"

"Survival"

DeAndre lowered his head. "What does a man with life in prison have to survive for?"

Gator smiled. "Kick it with me. I'll show you."

FOUR

DeAndre was working out when Keyvon knocked on his cell door around noon. The basketball game a few days before jarred him back to a semblance of his old self. He awoke every morning with his body craving physical exertion. Pushups. Crunches, Body squats. Mountain climbers. All became his breakfast. Five hundred of each in the confines of his cell. He was dripping a puddle when he opened the door for Keyvon.

"Gator wants you to come kick-it with him."

DeAndre frowned. "He sleeps on the third floor." He hadn't been in prison long, but he knew that getting caught in an unauthorized area was grounds for a disciplinary infraction. "Why can't he see me during yard call?"

"He don't want to see you during yard call. He wants to see you now." Kevon sniffed DeAndre's musty call and wrinkled his nose. "I'll wait for you to shower first."

DeAndre didn't think that he had a choice.

Twenty minutes later they were climbing up a concrete stairwell to the third floor. DeAndre had been moved to the WRB, the Work and Recreation Building, after he'd been assigned as a janitor two days before. Gator also lived in WRB, but DeAndre hadn't seen him since his one-on-one with Bull. He was never on the yard. Never in the chow hall. The man was a ghost.

They exited the stairwell inside H-Block, one of two housing dorms on the third floor. Keyvon walked out into a lobby where two female officers sat behind a desk. DeAndre stopped before leaving the block, knowing that he could get into trouble if he crossed that threshold.

Keyvon turned back. "Come on, man."

The women looked at DeAndre. One of them was Officer Martin, the female who had taken his fingerprints when he first processed into prison. She waved a little when she saw him, but only so that he would notice. Her gesture coaxed him into the lobby.

He wanted to say something as he walked past, but it wasn't a good time. Maybe she was in training. She dropped her eyes from his. He wasn't sure if the guard that she sat with could be trusted. Or his presence may have been a reminder of the last time they were together. She had been weak and vulnerable then. He didn't know. And he had no intentions to push the issue. If she wanted to talk to him, she would find a way.

The entire G-Block was thick with a lingering cloud of marijuana smoke. Keyvon seemed not notice. He headed upstairs to the second tier where three men stood outside the open doorway of a cell in the corner. DeAndre followed without question.

Gator was inside the cell sitting on the edge of the bunk. He held a fat cigar in his grip billowing thick blue smoke. One other man was inside, laughing at something Gator had said.

Gator saw DeAndre standing in the doorway. "Schoolboy! C'mon and let me curse you out for a while."

DeAndre stayed put. If the guards came in and made a round, he could go to the hole for being in another con's cell. Keyvon picked up on his hesitation and pushed him inside.

"I saw you play on TV a dozen times," Gator was saying. "But there's nothing like seeing greatness in the flesh."

"I was just playing my game. Bull was top heavy. He couldn't keep up with me if I'd been wearing lead weights on my ankles."

Gator smiled. His eyes were low and glassy. "Humility is overrated. If you're that dude, own it. No need to be modest around me." DeAndre just stood there wondering what the purpose of this meeting was. Gator held out the blunt to DeAndre. "Smoke with me."

DeAndre shook his head. "I'm good." He had never ingested a drug in his life. He drank sometimes in college. Occasionally. He'd always been self-conscious of his bode. His future depended on his health. He didn't expect Gator to understand.

Gator stood to confront him. "You ain't gonna smoke with me?"

The other guy in the cell stepped closer. "Want me to eat him?"

Gator waved him off. "This ain't got nothing to do with you." He sucked his teeth and stared deep into DeAndre's eyes. "I'm going to give you some good advice about prison. When somebody wants to give you something, you should take it, because most people won't give you shit."

DeAndre's eyes bounced between the other guy and Gator's. "I don't smoke."

As Gator stared at him his head slithered slightly like a serpent; a snake; a King Cobra. A slow smile spread just before he passed the blunt to the other man. "The athletes, right?" DeAndre nodded. "Walk with me."

DeAndre followed Gator out of the smoky cell and down the mezzanine away from his crew. Gator leaned on the metal banister and wouldn't say anything until DeAndre did the same.

"Listen DeAndre. I didn't want to tell you this, but some people want to move on you."

"Move on me? You mean hurt me?" Gator nodded. "A lot of guys don't like how that girl died. They want to teach you a lesson."

"But I didn't kill her. I got convicted on a bunch of lies."

Gator waved his arm out over the cellblock below them. A few men were watching TV. A group sat around a table playing seven-card poker. Two guys were hunched over a chessboard. "Look around you, "Gator said." Ain't a soul in here guilty except in the eyes of God. Nobody cares about your innocence when they're sticking you full of holes for glory. When that happens, it ain't about you. It's about the name they can make for themselves. That's how shallow they are."

DeAndre didn't understand the mind of one who used violence as a fool. "Tell me who it is. I'll talk to them."

Gator snorted. "You a diplomat? Think you can negotiate with savages? A lion kills for blood and meat. Men kill for blood and money. Ain't much difference."

A knot twisted in DeAndre's belly. "What am I supposed to do? Die?"

"If you were standing alone, you'd have to move on them first, show them that you won't go down so easily. That's how Ray Carruth did it. They tested him. Stole some ink pins from him or something, just to see what he would do. Yeah. He showed them why he was drafted to the NFL made them airlift a dude out of here. Had him slurping mashed potatoes through a straw for six months." Gator chuckled at the memory. "But you you're not alone."

"I'm not?"

"Nah. I already put the word out. The man who puts his hands on you won't live to tell about it. If anybody violates, we'll paint the walls red."

DeAndre wondered what Gator had seen in his life that allowed him to speak of death and killing so easily. That and what had he done that gave him the power to order such a thing. DeAndre had never been in the presence of royalty, but in that moment, he saw Gator not as a convict, but as a king with his word as a crown.

DeAndre had to look away. He held no admiration in his eyes for what Gator had done no matter how necessary it was and he was afraid his gaze would betray him. One of the chess players glanced up at him. The locked eyes for a second. Long enough for DeAndre to wonder if he was one of the men who wanted to hurt him. The man looked back to his game.

"I appreciate you standing up for me, but I'll handle it myself." DeAndre said.

Gator spun around and leaned his back against the rail. "You can't punch a hole in a wet paper bag. Even the weakest in here sees that. You're a baller and a scholar. Play your position. See that's where young brothers go wrong in here. They try to be more than what they are and get swallowed up in the storm. Don't try to meet force with force. Just be you."

"Yeah, but I don't want to owe you anything."

"Owe me?"

"Your protection can't be free."

Gator laughed. "We only extort white boys. You don't owe me anything."

"What you want me to join your gang?"

Gator smacked his lips. "You've been watching too many prisons-shows on TV. I couldn't bring you home. The relationship would change. You couldn't be your own man. You're smart. Keyvon and them are smart too, but not like you. Like when you wouldn't smoke with me. Most dudes would have sucked down the blunt just because I told them to. You know what you are and aren't willing to do. That's your strength."

The female guards entered to make a round. They headed to the bottom tier first. Gator looked over to Keyvon and the others standing around his cell door. "Y'all get missing." They started down the stairs." "Not you Keyvon. Hawk the man."

Keyvon didn't leave the cell block with the others. He went to the bottom tier and sat at an empty table in the front with a view out into the lobby.

DeAndre asked Gator, "So you don't want me to do anything in return?"

"Nothing that you wouldn't be willing to do."

"What do you mean?"

"Every summer we have a basketball tournament. Biggest in the state. You just missed the last one. I lost five-hundred dollars, but with you, I could win five thousand."

The pressure in DeAndre's belly eased a bit. "You want me to play ball on your team."

"That's right."

"I can do that."

The females were on the top tier now heading toward DeAndre and Gator. The girl with Martin was shorter, about five 'four with thick thighs and an under average face. DeAndre noticed that both of her front pockets were bulging. She stopped right in front of Gator.

He smiled her way. "Officer Johnson. What do you have going on today?"

Johnson held up a pair of limp latex gloves. "Gotta search your cell."

"You know where it is."

Martin mouthed, "Hey." To DeAndre as she walked past him towards Gator's cell in the corner.

Johnson turned to Martin. "Let me get this one alone. Just hang out here for a few minutes."

Martin stopped and watched Johnson and Gator enter his cell. The door closed behind them.

DeAndre stepped beside her. "Do you know what she's doing?"

Martin shook her head slowly. "I don't think I want to know. She's not supposed to be in an inmate's cell alone."

DeAndre could think of nothing to say that would set her at ease. "I don't want you to get in trouble."

"Me neither. Jobs don't sprout like weeds. Most of the good ones are taken."

"Keep looking," he said. "This place isn't for you."

"Is that right?"

"Yeah."

"What about you?" She gestured toward Gator's closed cell door. "I've heard all about him. His name is all over this prison. What are you doing with him?"

"I'm not with him. He's, uh he's helping me out."

Martin slid in closer. "Be careful, DeAndre. I know what they convicted you for doing. I don't care about that. You're a good man. Don't let this place or these people turn you into something you're not."

"Martin..."

"Promise me," she said.

"I promise."

"Good. If you need something, let me know. I won't bring you drugs, but I'll help you if I can."

Johnson came out of Gator's cell and told Martin, "All done."

DeAndre noticed that Johnson's pockets were now flat and empty.

As the girls turned to leave, Martin whispered to DeAndre, "Remember what I said."

DeAndre watched them exit the block. After they left, he spotted Kevon looking at him with his eyebrows bunched. He looked to Martin, then back to DeAndre.

Gator was right. Kevon was smart. Too smart.

CHAPTER
FIVE

eAndre didn't see the shiv in his attacker's hand at first. He was doing his best to dodge punches, or so he thought. Which was a hard thing to do in the narrow stairwell.

He and Gator had gone to the canteen. They were headed upstairs, their arms loaded with bags of chips, sodas, and hygiene items, when the dark-skinned dread pounced on them from above.

The guy went straight at DeAndre, no reason, no cause. He brought his clenched fist down in an arching swipe aimed like a hammer at DeAndre's face. DeAndre dropped his food bags and latched onto the dread's wrists. They danced in a tight circle, muscle's bulging and firm. The Dread slammed DeAndre's back into the concrete wall.

His attacker's eyes were wide and bulging out of his head, his teeth gritted tight like blood thirsty vampire fangs. The two men were a pair of snuffing breaths and expended effort. Dread kneed DeAndre in the groin. DeAndre recoiled enough for the man to wedge his forearm into DeAndre's throat to keep him still. DeAndre kept a firm grip on the other wrist, which was inches from his face. That's when he saw the thick sliver of plastic sharpened to a deadly point.

DeAndre took his eyes from the immediate threat long enough to look for Gator. He was lounging against a wall with his arms crossed, palms tucked into his arm pits, watching. DeAndre tried to yell for help, but the word would not come.

Dread tried to yank his wrist out of DeAndre's grip. He did it over and over to break DeAndre down. DeAndre held on, though he felt the angel of death cradle his heart in its cold bony hand. A part of him knew that he could fight the guy all day, but he wasn't sure if he wanted to. What did he have to live for?

He saw himself as a six-year-old boy. His mother had given him a basketball for his birthday. And then, he was in a park practicing jump shots. Summer turned to fall. Fall to winter. He was still in the park, shooting in rain, snow, and sunshine.

He saw himself grow tall and strong, conquering the trials and tribulations of life. These images snatches of his existence flashed before his eyes in less than a millisecond. His mother's kiss. Teammates hoisting him on their shoulders after a game-winning shot. The day he announced that he would play for NC State. Milestones flooded his mind in hazy glimpses that he wished to relive again. Even the moment when his best friend Michael brought a gun into a party. A gun that had killed Tabitha. He saw the faces of the jury, hateful and full of vengeance. He heard the judges gravel bang down, and the word, "Guilty" echo throughout the courtroom.

And then darkness. For the light of his past had been overshadowed by his black future. All his hard work, the practice, and his lifelong dedication to basketball was pointless. He was going to die in prison.

Dread-head jerked his wrist back, and DeAndre let go. He saw the knife slicing through the air on a course for his beating heart. He closed his eyes to welcome death, but the blow never came.

The forearm was snatched from his throat. DeAndre hunched over, gasping for breath. He looked up to see an older guy with a bald head and beard fighting his attacker. Dread swung the shiv at the elder con in the same way that he had swung it at Andre. The old head blocked the blow at Dread's wrist and latched onto his arm. He launched an elbow to Dread's jaw, then wrenched his arm backward. Dred hollered in pain. The shiv clattered to the concrete landing. Seconds later, the shiv clattered to the concrete landing and Dread went bouncing down the stairs too. He landed face down, motionless.

Winded, the older guy grabbed DeAndre and pulled him up the stairs. "We need to get out of here before somebody finds him."

Dark blood pooled around Dread's head. DeAndre followed the guy, taking three steps at a time. Two flights up he stopped and turned back. "Where's Gator?"

"Gator?" The old man questioned. "That sucker has been gone. Come on. What floor do you sleep on?"

Gator left him. The thought seemed unfathomable. "I just moved to the third floor, H-Block."

They started moving again.

On the third floor, DeAndre hurried to his cell and collapsed on his bunk. "Thanks for helping me. I don't know your name."

"Preach. Everybody calls me, Preach."

DeAndre sat up and looked at him. He'd seen Preach before. He was always playing chess with another older guy. "Okay, Preach. I'd be dead if it wasn't for you."

Preach shook his head. "Didn't have anything to do with me. The Lord put me in that stairwell at that moment. So, don't thank me. Thank Him."

DeAndre nodded. "I will. I promise."

Preach didn't leave. He stood there starring down on DeAndre. "Listen, man. I don't know what you've got going on, but you need to watch the company you keep. This dude Gator, I've known him for years. Everybody around him either ends up locked up or dead, but somehow he always gets away clean."

DeAndre ran a hand down his face, still trembling from adrenaline. "Gator isn't the problem. He's been helping me."

Preach frowned. "Helping you how?"

"Looking out. Keeping the goons off me."

"Yeah, I can see that. Some Negro just tried to hit you with a pig sticker eight inches long while that fool leaned against the wall watching. Looked like a whole lot of help to me."

You don't you don't understand." DeAndre stood, realizing that Preach was right, but not wanting to admit it. He just wanted to be alone so he could think. "Why are you up in my business anyway?"

"I'm trying to put you up on game."

"I don't know you, bro."

Preach stepped inside DeAndre's cell. "You don't have to know me to see who's on your side and who isn't. The truth is in your face. But you have to want to see it."

DeAndre's fists curled at his side.

Preach noted DeAndre's aggressive posture. "So, you gonna fight me now?" DeAndre didn't respond. He held up his empty palms. "I'll leave but let me apologize first. You're right. We don't know each other. And I don't want you to think that I'm coming down on you, because I'm not. You've been through enough today."

"Tell me about it."

"Let that be your wake-up call."

"Wake-up call for what?"

Preach chose his words carefully. "Proverbs twenty-four, one and two: Be not thou envious against evil men, neither desire to be with them. For their heard studies destruction, and their lips talk of mischief."

DeAndre frowned. "What is that supposed to mean?"

"There are a lot of ways to do time. If you start out wrong, you'll always be wrong. Then years later, if you want to change, you've got to live with the damage already done in your youth. Take it from me, young blood. Some damage can't be repaired. But if you start out right, this life will be easier."

"You're talking in riddles, Preach."

"No, I'm not. I'm saying that if you were living right, you wouldn't need someone to protect you. All you would need is the Lord. Trust him, and he will be your protector."

"Gator..."

Preach shook his head. "I'm not just talking about Gator..."

DeAndre pointed to the cell door behind Preach. He turned to see Gator standing with six men behind him.

Gator told Preach, "You put in some pretty work down in that stairwell. It's good to see that the old man still has it." Preach just stared at him. "Now get missing. Ain't no pulpit for convicts here."

"I ain't looking for a pulpit, young man. Just salvation. As should you."

Gator flashed a half smile. "God is a fairy tale for women and children."

"No, son. God is the giving light that will lead you to a better life."

Gator laughed this time. "What a life God gave me. A life of concrete and steel."

"Try prayer. He'll deliver you if it is his will."

"You pray, don't you? But you're in this cage with me. Why doesn't he deliver you?" Preach let out a long sigh.

"God's plan is never wrong, wherever it leads me."

"I ain't here to hold a philosophical discussion." Gator stepped aside to give Preach room to walk out.

Preach got the message. He turned to DeAndre. "Remember what I said. I'll be around if you need me."

DeAndre didn't respond. He watched Preach leave his cell.

"Give us a minute, "Gator told his boys, then stepped into DeAndre's cell and closed the door.

"You left me, Gator. That dude could have killed me."

"I didn't leave you. Preach was fighting the guy. Looked like both y'all could have handled it. I had to go get my people."

"Say what you want. You weren't trying to fight." DeAndre remembered Gator leaning against the wall with his arms crossed, trying not to get his hands dirty. "You just stood there."

"DeAndre..."

"I'm not buying it. You front like you're so hard so though. But you're not. You're..." Gator rushed DeAndre and shove him against the wall. He pressed the sharpened point of a steel shank to DeAndre's throat. "Don't tell me what I am and what I ain't. It's not my fault you can't scrap. If you want to know the truth, I wanted to see what you would do under pressure, how you'd handle yourself. I wasn't going to let him do you. I would have stopped him before...."

"You were afraid, and you know it."

Gator's lips pulled back in a sneer as he bared his fangs. He pressed the knife harder into DeAndre's throat, then let it fall limply to his side. He huffed out a hot breath and stepped away.

"Believe what you want. That's over now. So, I don't care. But you've got a decision to make."

DeAndre rubbed his throat where the knife stung his flesh. "A decision about what?"

"I'm sending Keyvon to eat the dude that tried to do you."

"He's okay?"

"They say he got up and walked away like nothing happened." He studied DeAndre. "Do you want to do it yourself? You don't have to cut him. Kevon will make sure nobody jumps in."

DeAndre sat heavily on his bed. He buried his face in his hands, remembering the Dread's hot breath beating against his cheek as he struggled to stab DeAndre. "Why can't you just let it be?" He asked Gator.

Ain't no such thing. If you violate, you get dealt with. This is prison. That's how it is. You can't just pick up and move to another neighborhood. You've got to look that man in his face every day and remember what he tried to do to you. And, he has to ask himself when you'll try for some get back. Sooner or later it'll go down again. That's why you can't let it be. You've got to kill it before it kills you."

DeAndre stared at the floor in thought. "I'm not going."

Gator nodded. "I didn't think you would, but that's a good thing. I know a lot of lambs pretending to be lions. We always find out the truth in the end. At least you know who you are and how far you're willing to go." He strutted out. Before closing DeAndre's cell door, Gator turned back. "If you ever call me a coward again, I'll kill you."

It was quiet long after Gator left. The only sounds were the chaotic thoughts in DeAndre's head. He wasn't built for prison life. He wanted to be strong to be the fighter that he needed to be for survival, but he knew that he didn't have it in him.

There was a soft knock at his door. He saw Officer Martin through the small window. She pulled the cell door open. "You okay?"

DeAndre wanted to lie to her. "No."

She peered around the cellblock to make sure no one was watching before she eased into his cell. "What's wrong, DeAndre?"

"It's nothing."

She sat on his bunk. When he stared at the floor to avoid her gaze, she lifted his chin with her fingers. Instead of asking him again, she wrapped her arms around him.

DeAndre leaned into her, sobbing and trembling.

CHAPTER
SIX

DeAndre hated the non-contact visits at Central Prison. The visiting booth was no more than a six-by-six cube with a hard steel stool on the prison side. A floor-to-ceiling wall with a small rectangular window was his only link to the outside.

He stepped into the booth and sat down. An officer closed the door and locked him inside. Twenty minutes later his mother, Jolene, exited an elevator with four or five other visitors. She wore a tan business suit, matching heels and a frown.

Jolene didn't see him as she entered. She stepped out of his line of sight to check in at the officer's station. A moment later she swung open his door and walked in with her nose sniffing the air. Her eyes scrutinized every surface before laying a finger on anything.

DeAndre put on his best smile. "Hello, Jolene." She had insisted that he call her Jolene, instead of mama, to make her appear younger to people that didn't know them.

Jolene glanced at him with one eyebrow raised. "I hate coming here." She eyed the plastic chair on her side as if she could see each bacterial microbe slithering around on the surface. With caution she finally sat, then smiled as if seeing him for the first time. "DeAndre. You've lost weight. Are you getting the money I've been sending? I know that you need it, but I have been hesitant because I don't trust these people…" Her eyes narrowed. "No one is taking your money, are they?" She leaned in close to the glass. "They aren't trying to mess with you?"

He laughed a little. "No Ma. Nobody is trying to mess with me. I'm losing weight because they don't have free weights here. I've been running a lot. Besides that, I don't eat much. All they serve is processed meat and a ton of carbs. I'm living off of beans and mackerel."

"Be careful of the packaged fish, it's loaded with salt. High-blood pressure runs in the family. Your grandfather had it so bad that he was eating wet tree bark because he couldn't handle anything else." She took a moment to appraise him. "So, no one is extorting you? Everything is okay?" DeAndre took his time to answer. "It's as okay as it can be."

"I know baby, "she admitted. Jolene looked away so that he wouldn't see the tear fall from her eye. When she gained her courage to face him, she asked, "Your appeal?"

"I lost."

"Already?" What's it been, six months?" He didn't respond. "Why didn't you tell me sooner? We've spoken on the phone several times."

"I didn't want to think about it. I got the opinion last month. My lawyer filed a petition for Discretionary Review, but…"

"Slow down. What's that?"

"A Petition for Discretionary Review is my last chance to win in North Carolina. After that, I'll have to file a Federal Habeas Corpus."

Jolene shifted uneasily in her seat. "What did your lawyer say after he filed the Petition thing? Does he think you have a chance to get out?"

DeAndre held her gaze for an eternity. He hated that she had to visit him in such a place. At this time in his life she should have been helping Tabitha pick out a wedding gown and helping decorate their new house. Neither of them ever thought life would bring them to this setting. A prison. He'd been a straight A student since the day he walked into a school for the first time, because she sat down and helped him with his homework every night that she could. She had expected him to be an overachiever because she knew his potential and expected nothing less. To look her in the face through a hazy glass window made him wish he was dead instead of locked up.

He shook his head. "He said it was a long shot at best."

"What can you do then?"

DeAndre shrugged. "He's court-appointed. He didn't have to file the petition. At that point, his job was already done."

Jolene sat for a moment, thinking. "They should have to do more. Society doesn't care about young black men like you. They have no problem locking you up forever. But when one of theirs commits a crime, 'oh he was an angel who only messed up this once.' It's not fair. The system is not fair. Young black men are getting shot down in the street by the police who swore to protect them. And who cares? Nobody. On top of that, while society loads up a go-fund-me for the murderer's legal defense fund. Why? All because he shot an innocent, unarmed black man. And you don't even have a lawyer willing to take you one step further."

"Ma, nobody is going to do something for free. If you had hired a post-conviction attorney when I asked you to, I might be home already."

"It's my fault now? I didn't kill anybody."

"Neither did I."

"DeAndre, your best friend got on the stand and testified that he saw you with a gun, and say you ..."

"DeAndre slapped the glass separating them. "He was lying!"

Jolene slammed back into her seat, reeling from his anger. Then she realized that a wall was between them, and he could do nothing to her. "Why didn't you testify? That's what innocent people do."

"I shouldn't have had to testify, "he said. "Michael shouldn't have lied." They sat there, breathing hard, calming down.

Finally, Jolene said, "If that's the case, then he'll have to answer to God."

"I can't wait that long. I need to get another lawyer now."

"How much money do you think I make, DeAndre? Your trial lawyer cost me two-fifty. That's more than most people's houses cost, and I'm still paying it off. A guarantee that you would come home. Instead you're here, serving life. I got no refund, DeAndre. You're spending forty-five dollars a week for food and deodorant. I get you books, magazines, sneakers, and whatever else your little ungrateful heart desires. Yet you want me to cough up another twenty-five thousand for an appeal lawyer? Supporting you is putting me in the poor house. I cannot spend every dime that I make on you.

DeAndre felt the adrenaline pumping through his veins, and it was a struggle to keep his anger in check. "Ma, you don't understand how this works."

"Oh, I know how it works. You'll beg and beg until I give in. You'll pester me until I can't stand it. It's what you've been doing since you were old enough to walk. But I've got news for you. This isn't a Nintendo game. I cannot spend money that I don't have. I am tapped out."

"Ma...."

"But if just if... you can get out... you haven't played basketball in almost two years. If you get out, there isn't an NBA team that would spit on you."

"I'm still healthy."

"You're labeled a murderer. That will never go away. Face the facts."

DeAndre didn't know how to respond. He sat there seething in the truth. "I understand what you're saying, but why do you have to be so negative?"

I'm not being negative, boy. I'm being real." She watched DeAndre stand up and pace the small room. "I raised you on my own..."

"So, it's my fault that my father died?"

Jolene reeled back as if she'd been slapped. "No, your father's absence is not your fault."

Why do you always throw it in my face as if it is? I grew up watching you struggle. I know how hard your life was. How do you think I felt watching you drag in from your second job, and then study for a college degree? All so that I could have a pair of Jorden's to hoop with."

Tears trickled down her cheeks. "I hate seeing you in here. I hate it even more that I can't do anything about it. I can't save you from this, DeAndre. Whether you're guilty or innocent. You'll have to find a way to save yourself."

The cool October wind swooped down into the concrete bowl that was Central Prison's yard, and it put a shiver in DeAndre's bones. He kept shooting the ball, ignoring the chill. He worked his way around the key, shouting at the apex of every two lines. After making it all the way around, he went to the three-point line and popped off shots every two feet.

NBA season would be starting soon. He'd read that his friend and roommate, Michael Arrington, was entering his second year with the Milwaukee Bucks'. He'd signed a thirty-million-dollar contract.

DeAndre tried not to think about it, to think about Michael, or the fact that Michael was the reason that DeAndre was serving life. If it wasn't for Michael, DeAndre would be signing his own thirty-million-dollar contract.

He missed three shots in a row and knew that he'd tired himself out. He sat on the bleachers staring up at the gunmetal grey cloud cover, relishing the warm sweat dripping off his forehead.

Preach and his friend Percy stepped out on the yard. Percy carried an ancient chess set, the board fading, and the pieces in a filmy plastic bag. Preach spotted DeAndre and told Percy to set the board up. He'd be with him in a minute. "Don't take all damn day, "Percy responded.

Preach stepped to DeAndre on the bleachers. "You doing alright?"

DeAndre rolled his eyes. "I was." Preach didn't take the hint. DeAndre asked him, "What do you want"

"Peace."

DeAndre smirked. "I don't remember declaring war."

"We're at war with ourselves every day that we walk this earth. Man's struggle has always been to conquer himself."

DeAndre leaned back on the bleachers to get comfortable. "All you're missing is a church and congregation."

"I ain't preaching a sermon, some. I'm just telling the truth how it should be told."

"You act like you're trying to save me from some great harm. I'm good."

Preach kicked his foot up on the bottom bleacher. "Are you really good?"

"I'm making it."

"You're treading water and sinking fast."

"I don't need you to judge me. I'm my own man."

"Not the man that you could be."

DeAndre slid off the bleachers and faced Preach. "I didn't ask for your advice, and I don't need it."

"Sooner or later you'll realize just how much you do."

The gym door opened. Gator, Keyvon, and six other men waked out. They all shook hands with DeAndre.

Gator approached Preach and stood firm with his hands clasped in front of him. "Deacon. We keep crossing paths. If you're not careful we might bump heads."

Preach look him dead in the eye. "I ain't looking for trouble, but if it should come my way, 'Blessed be the Lord my strength which teaches my hands to war, and my fingers to fight:"

"Uh-huh," Gator mumbled. "That a Bible verse?"

"Psalms one-forty-four, verse one."

"I like that one. Might say it to one of my enemies."

"Don't play with the Lord, Gator."

"I can't play with something that doesn't exist."

Preach laughed and shook his head. "I'll be on my way."

"That might be a good thing."

Preach looked to DeAndre as he turned to leave but didn't say anything. He walked right past him.

Gator pulled DeAndre to the side. "Everything good?"

DeAndre nodded while staring after Preach, now sitting across from Percy to play chess. "What's up with you and him, Gator?"

"I met Preach when I first started doing time. About eighteen years ago. We were at Scotland Correctional. It was a warzone back then. I'm talking about stabbings every day. Brothers cliqued up. Sets started fighting for control. It was crazy."

"Preach survived through that by spitting Bible verses?"

Gator chuckled. "He wasn't always the Pope, Schoolboy. Preach used to get it in. He owned all the poker games on the yard, to Parle tickets, he ran reefer. And held it down by himself. He hustled without a team, and nobody tried him. Everybody knew that Preach would cut you quicker than you could breathe."

DeAndre looked across the yard at Preach again, remembering how he'd saved him in the stairwell. "You respected him too?"

"I worked for him. He was the first con on state to put a pound of weed in my hands. He had it. We had no choice but to respect him."

"So, what happened?"

"The East Coast Bloods. They took over everything. It was get down or lay down. See, Preach was a hustler who would hurt you if he had to. This new breed they weren't about equal opportunity. They took and took, then they stabbed you if you wouldn't give it to them. I never saw nothing like it. I got in with them because I saw down the line."

"What happened to Preach? Did y'all put him out of business?"

"Nah. He just quit hustling. Never gave a reason. One week, he was the most rugged dude on the yard. The next, he was going to church and leading Bible studies. He changed and never looked back." Gator studied DeAndre. "Did you see the light on the road to Damascus or something?"

"Just curious."

"Don't be," Gator warned. "Prison breaks the strongest dudes in half, twists them around and does it again. Most are lucky if they change for the better. I still respect him. He had the courage to do the one thing most of us can't."

"What's that?"

"Start living right." Gator watch DeAndre for a minute. "You look a little lost."

"I had a visit. Came out here to get some air and work off some aggression."

"I'm glad to hear that. I got a guy who thinks he can beat you one-on-one. I put up four packs of cigs. You ready?"

DeAndre looked off. The last thing he wanted to do was play for money. He wanted to go to his cell and crawl under the covers. He told Gator, "Yeah, I'm ready."

***

Percy scrutinized the chess board. His hand hovered above a piece but hesitated to move it. Finally, he moved the piece. "Check mate."

Preach sat back heavily. "You won again."

"What's up with you, sukkah? That's four games straight."

"Not my day, Percy. You better enjoy it."

"Oh, I will, but I don't like winning that way. You've got something weighing on your mind. What is it?" Preach shrugged, then he started setting up the board again. "Preach. It's that boy, ain't it? What is it about him that makes you get out of character?"

Preach looked over at DeAndre playing basketball. "I see a lot of me in him, and I wish that I didn't."

Gator paced back and forth in his cell bare-chested. Gang tattoos blanked his upper torso like some yakuza mob boss. He squinted from the smoking blunt dangling from his mouth. "So, I get out of the car and this big-ass rooster runs up to me and started pecking my leg. It's me, my man Beans, and Terrell. Now, Beans had been cupping big eights and quarter keys of powder from the Mexican whose trailer it was. Amigo never ran out. The plan was to creep to the door, kick it in, and get the drop on him before he knows what's going on. But this damn chicken had other plans." "Gator took a hard hit off his blunt and held the smoke in his lungs.

Kevon and Deadman, another one of Gator's cronies sat on Gator's bunk laughing. DeAndre chuckled some but wasn't high like the others.

"I grew up in Detroit, "Gator continued. "I never saw a chicken unless it was frozen or on a plate with extra crispy skin. When I moved to Charlotte that was the city too. They didn't have any chicken farms on West Boulevard, feel me."

Deadman laughed so hard that he could barely breathe. "You was scared?"

Gator cocked one eyebrow his way. "Scared? Negro, I was petrified." He held a hand, palm down, next to his waist. "The damn thing was this tall, bro. I didn't know they made chickens that big."

"What'd you do?" Kevon asked him.

"There wasn't much that I could do. I had this big AK in my hands, and I'm trying to keep that down so nobody will call the cops, but this big-ass damn chicken keeps nipping at my legs. I kicked him. He kind of flew backwards, then he came right back, flapping his wings."

Deadman reached for the blunt. "What were your homeboys doing?"

Gator took one last hit and passed it. "Laughing. Like y'all stupid asses right now. But we couldn't stand out there all night. I told B and Terrell to post up by the door. When I walked over there, the chicken stayed in front of me, biting me and running away. When I got to the door, I whispered for Terrell to kick it in. He pointed to the chicken. I told him to do it anyway. So Terrell kicks in the door. The chicken jumped high and flew at my face. I raised the chopper and blasted him into the living room, right into Amigo's lap. He had so much chicken blood splattered over him that I thought he was shot."

Dedicated to the blunt, Deadman hit it while laughing so hard that he choked.

Kevon snatched the blunt from him.

"Amigo was so scared that he gave it all up. "Gator said. "Every crumb. We left with two-and-a-half birds and fifty thousand in cash. Best lick of my life."

Deadman asked, "Did you take the chicken with you?"

Gator took the blunt. "I would have, but I didn't know how to pluck it. Trust me, I wanted to eat him after all the trouble he caused me." He hit the blunt. "We went to Bojangles after that. Ate his brother instead with a side of dirty rice."

DeAndre gave a half-smile while Kevon and Deadman cracked up.

"Ain't nobody gonna play me. "Gator said. "Not a dude nor a chicken. Nobody."

Keyvon and Deadman were having the time of their lives. They'd been hanging in Gator's cell the whole afternoon, letting endless hours slink by while listening to Gator's wild tales. He told a million of them; club fights, drive-byes, and robberies. Keyvon and Deadman nodded then laughed at all the appropriate places. They kept their eyes locked on Gator, studying his every move, never missing a movement.

The only thing DeAndre had in common with them was that they were all serving life without parole. He could not relate to the stories Gator told. They were so far from the life he knew that he could not picture the scenes in his mind's eyes. The situations they envied left DeAndre puzzled and horrified. How could one man be so bad?

Most of the convicts that DeAndre met were black and under thirty like him, but he did not understand them. The longer that he remained in Gator's cell, the more he wanted to leave.

He remembered days long done when he was a freshman at State. Ten of them would be crowded in a dorm room playing video games. Kevon and Deadman would feel out of place in his world, as he did in theirs. What was worse was that none of the young black men he met were trying to get out of prison. They never spoke of the law or getting back into court. They smoked weed, told war stories, and found ways to be comfortable in prison. They had given up. They were dead to the real world as insignificant as the chicken Gator had killed so mercilessly.

"Schoolboy," Gator said, his eyes low. "Bull said he's getting a team together to take you down. He wants to run a game and try to win his money back."

DeAndre shook his head. "I'm not feeling it today." He had played several games over the last few days, and he needed a rest. "Besides, you haven't paid me for the first game when I beat Bull. You haven't paid me anything...ever."

Gator gritted his teeth. "Pay you?" He looked to Keyvon and Deadman who were no longer laughing. "You hear him?" He asked them.

DeAndre hesitated. "You said that you were going to give me half of what you won. I haven't seen a nickel."

He wouldn't have mentioned it if he had money. Necessity gave him courage. His mom had stopped sending him money. He couldn't complain because he knew that she was hurting. It wasn't her fault that he was locked up and understanding his mother's financial situation didn't make life easier for DeAndre. He made forty cents a day as a janitor. Most canteen items cost double his weekly salary. Without some kind of hustle, he could not survive. Something had to give. He didn't like the idea of having to sell cigarettes, but there was nothing else that he could do.

"I'll pay you," Gator told DeAndre. "You've got to be patient though."

I've been patient. It's been six months since that first game. Don't tell me you haven't been paid yet."

"What are you trying to say, Schoolboy? That I don't keep my word?" Gator approached him. "I needed that money to make something bigger happen. That's what I'm waiting on now. When it pops off, I'll tighten you up. But until then, I need you to strap up and hit the court."

DeAndre looked deep into his eyes. "I'm not playing."

Gator snatched him by the front of the shirt and slammed him into the wall.

Out of sheer reflex, DeAndre shoved him away. Gator was so high that he stumbled. DeAndre swung on him before he could think better of it. Gator was still falling when Kevon and Deadman attacked DeAndre.

Deadman's arching right hook caught him straight in the eye. DeAndre's head bounced off the concrete wall. Keyvon swept his legs out from under him. When he hit the ground, they stomped on him. DeAndre curled into a ball to protect his head.

Gator got to his feet. "Let him up."

Keyvon and Deadman stopped kicking him and back away. Gator stood over him looking down. "You can't put your hands on me, Schoolboy. Get up." DeAndre uncovered his head and peeked out. "Ain't nobody gonna bother you. Get up"

DeAndre climbed to his feet. He felt a sharp pain in his ribs and hunched over, clutching his abdomen.

"You alright?" Gator reached out to him.

DeAndre recoiled toward the door. "Don't touch me." He backed out.

"Schoolboy!" Gator called out as DeAndre headed toward the stairwell.

As he stumbled down the stairs, he heard Gator telling his boys, "Why y'all beat him like that? Now how is he going to make me some money?"

Officer Martin was sitting at the officer's desk in the lobby when DeAndre hurried out. She called to him, but he kept walking.

DeAndre entered H-Block across the hall and went straight to his cell. When he laid down, it hurt to stretch out. He fingered his ribs. None of them felt broken, just tender. He curled up until the pain no longer hindered him.

No long after, Martin was at his door knocking. He didn't respond. She opened the door and frowned down on him. "Oh, so you don't know me anymore?"

"This isn't the time, Martin."

"You better make time." She craned her neck to get a better look at him. "What's wrong with your eye?"

"My eye?" DeAndre reached up and touched it. The flesh was swollen. His ribs hurt so bad that he hadn't noticed. He pulled his hand away." I'm okay. I-I fell down the stairs."

"You didn't fall down no damn stairs, so try something else." She entered his cell and knelt beside him. Her eyes roamed over his face. "You need to go to medical. Your eye is closing."

"I'm not going to medical."

"Stop being so prideful." She stood. "I'm calling the Sergeant."

DeAndre struggled to sit up. "Don't do that. He'll ask questions. I can't have that."

Martin thought about it. "What happened, DeAndre?"

He let out a long sigh. Couldn't stand to meet her eyes. "Martin..."

"Why don't you trust me?"

DeAndre looked up at her then. "It doesn't have anything to do with trust."

She stared down on him, shaking her head. "Look. I'm going on break in a few minutes. I'll try to bring you some ice."

Before she left, he said, "Don't tell anybody. Please."

She glanced back to him, her lips a thin line of frustration. "I won't." She left.

DeAndre laid down again, wondering how his life had ended up so horrible.

Martin returned thirty minutes later with a Ziploc bag stuffed with ice. She sat on the edge of his bed and made him hold the ice to his eye.

"You shouldn't stay, "he said. "Thanks for helping me, but I don't want to get you into trouble."

"DeAndre. I'm not leaving until I know you're okay. Johnson is out there. She'll let me know when I have to go."

"Can you trust her?"

She shrugged. "With all the dirt she's doing...I better be able to. I mean, it's not like we're doing anything. I'm just sitting here."

He was worried more about the pattern her presence created. She'd been a regular fixture around his cell since she was assigned to the housing unit. They had grown as close as an officer and a prisoner could in as safe a way as possible. All it took was for one snitch to make light of their familiarity and she would be moved to another unit.

DeAndre was in a bad spot, but he had never asked her for anything, and didn't plan on it. He didn't want to be the cause of her getting in trouble. He wouldn't be able to live with himself if that happened.

"Are you going to tell me what happened, or what?" She asked.

She smelled of wild berries and vanilla. Her hair was braided, thick braids, twisted into a hive on top of her head. He had never known a woman more beautiful. "No," he said. "Let me handle it."

"Is that right? I don't want to be picking you up off the floor the next time this happens."

"There won't be a next time."

"How can I be sure of that? You won't even tell me what happened."

"Let it go, Melody."

"I won't. You don't know who your friend is, and who's your enemy."

"I know," he said.

"I can't tell. You might not want to tell me what happened, but I bet that damn Gator had something to do with it."

DeAndre drummed his fists on his knees. "You don't know what you're talking about."

"I do. He sent one of his boys to me saying that he knew you and I had something going on, and if I didn't meet his cousin in Raleigh and get some drugs to bring to him, he would make trouble for you."

His fists clenched tighter. "What? Tell me you didn't."

"Hell no. But now this happens to you...." She gestured to his face. "And I'm thinking that I should have."

DeAndre clutched her hand. "Don't do that. What happened to me today had nothing to do with you."

"Don't lie to me, DeAndre."

"I'm not lying. I didn't know anything about that situation, but now that I do, I'm going to put a stop to it."

"How?" she asked.

"I don't know."

EIGHT

DeAndre asked around and found out that Preaches cell was on the second floor. By the time he'd gained the courage to see him, his rips were okay, and his eye was discolored but no longer swollen. He'd seen Gator and some of his boys, but none of them approached him. Though he was thankful for the peace, the impending confrontation was inevitable, like a cold or nightfall or death. It was just a matter of time.

Preach slept in cell two-thirteen. DeAndre knocked on the steel door without looking in so he wouldn't catch him in a compromising position. Preach peeked out of his square window and gave a knowing smile when he saw DeAndre standing there. He opened the door.

He squinted at DeAndre's black eye. "You get that playing ball?" DeAndre shook his head and looked down. "I didn't think so."

As hard as it was, DeAndre met Preaches eyes. He felt no shame for being here. His shame came from not showing up sooner.

Preach stepped back into his cell and sat down on his bed. DeAndre stood at the door. Preaches cell was spotless. The walls were white and ivory, without a speck of dust. The concrete floor was polished and waxed to a high sheen. His wall locker was open. Sparse possessions were aligned meticulously, evenly spaced and placed with perfection. Old pictures were taped to the open locker door in an overlapping collage. The biggest image caught DeAndre's eye. It was of a young boxer stooped in a fighting pose with huge red gloves on his small fists. The caption read: David "Dynamite" Harris vs. Charles Pridgen. Eight p.m. Below the wall locker was a stack of magazines and another stack of books, manila envelopes, and a yellow writing pad with notes scribbled in chicken scratch. The surface of the bed was the only area in disarray.

DeAndre shoved his chin toward the poster. "That you?"

Preach glanced at the picture, then nodded. "Long time ago." "Were you any good?"

"I won more than I lost. Knocked out a few. That was good enough for me."

This was the first time that DeAndre looked at him as a man, not through the hazy Kaleidoscopic lens of anger dancing with annoyance. Preaches beard was more gray than black, short and trimmed with angular lines. His black scalp was slick and bald. He was tall and firm from years of use. He looked better than a man half his age. The longer DeAndre looked at him, the more familiar Preach looked, like he had a face that DeAndre had seen before. He did not know why that feeling washed over him. He only knew that it did.

DeAndre gestured to the items covering the bed. "Did I catch you at a bad time?"

"Not really. Just studying some old case law."

"Law stuff? I need to do that too, but I haven't seen a law library around here."

"You won't. North Carolina got rid of their law libraries in the early eighties."

DeAndre raised his eyebrows. There were a lot of papers on his bed. "How did you get all those?"

"If a man wants something bad enough, he'll find a way to get it."

DeAndre thought about that and what Gator had said about him. How Preach used to be. "Have you ever helped anybody get out of prison?"

Preach studied DeAndre a long time before answering. "I got some guy's time cut. The most was ten years. That was a while back. I don't do much law work anymore. Only myself. Spent a lot of time helping everybody else. Never could get myself out, though."

"How long have you been down?"

"Twenty-one years."

DeAndre sighed. "Damn." He couldn't imagine being in prison for that long, even though he was destined for that future. "That's as long as I've been alive." Preach looked toward the wall. DeAndre spoke up so he wouldn't lose him. "Was it hard?"

"What, the time?" DeAndre nodded some. "Hell, yeah, it was hard. It's hard right now. It's hard every damned day. That's why I'm in here studying the law so I don't have to suffer anymore.

"But you've survived."

Preach stood and stepped to DeAndre. They were almost the same height. Preach was an inch or two shorter. His gaze tiptoed over DeAndre's black eye. "I survived by giving Caesar what belonged to Caesar until I realized that I only had God to answer to."

"The Bible?"

"Mathew twenty-two, twenty-one."

"What does it mean?"

"It means that when living on this earth we have to follow the laws of man to survive. In prison, follow the law of the system, and also the law of the convict. Violating either has its consequences. Sometimes we do things in prison that we don't want to do, for survival. It could be to have something to eat when you're hungry or to stay alive, period. I did the wrong things for a long time because I thought I had to to be happy. Luckily, I learned that I am not bound by the laws of man. Only by the word of God. As long as I live by his law, everything will be all right."

DeAndre felt like he had shrunk a foot shorter, felt that he was not fit to face such a man. He wondered if he would live long enough to have that type of wisdom. In prison he was a sprocket that had no function in the mechanical workings of the machine. While the other gears turned flawlessly, in tune with each other, his presence was jerky and unbalanced.

He was as out of place in prison as he was standing at Preaches door. "Well, sorry for bothering you." He turned away. "I'll go now."

"It's okay." Preach reached out and clasped his arm. "I didn't mean to run you off with the preaching."

"That's not it."

"What is it then? You showed up here for something."

He was right. DeAndre had showed up at his cell door for something. Yet he was unsure about what it was exactly. A part of him wanted to tell Preach about his situation with Gator, and how Gator tried to pressure Martin to bring him drugs. DeAndre knew that if anybody would understand, it would be Preach, but he couldn't bring himself to ask for advice. Instead, he said, "Will you teach me to fight?"

Preach glanced at the poster, then back to DeAndre. A slow smile spread across his lips. "No." He walked back to his bed and sat down. "I know you didn't come down here for that. You didn't even know."

"I didn't," he admitted. "I saw the poster, and I thought…"

"Why do you want to learn how to fight? Do you think being able to throw your hands will keep Gator off you?"

DeAndre reached up and fingered his black eye. "What makes you think Gator had something to do with this?"

"He probably didn't. If anything, he sent the order. Gator doesn't have to fight his own babbles anymore, and he doesn't want to. He's too smart to get his own hands dirty. That's his gift, intelligence. There are billionaires out there who don't have half the brains he does.

DeAndre shook his head. "Gator didn't…"

"Don't lie to me. You don't have to tell me what happened. But don't lie to me. I've been around too long. The game doesn't change in here, only the players."

"Well—how did you know Gator had something to do with it?"

"C'mon, man. You're a smart guy. Not many men in prison can say they have a college degree. Half don't even have a high school diploma. You're book smart. Gator he was raised in the streets. The drama your mama struggled to keep from killing you, was his teacher. He learned how ugly life could be before he knew what life was. Thriving in prison is natural to him. "Preach frowned and looked off like he'd been struck with a sharp pain that he could not control. "Just goes to show you how far or short a person can go with the only opportunities they were given. To the penthouse or the big house where you end up all depends on how you began."

DeAndre remembered living in rundown homes, hearing gunshots at night, and every face in his school being a black one. That was before his mother graduated from college and her new job swooped in like a magic carpet and whisked them from Chicago to North Carolina. The struggles he once knew faded into a memory so faint that it was like they had never happened at all. Where he had at one time hated Gator for what he did, he now understood why he did it.

Preach stood in a crouch and held up his fists like two steel mallets in front of his face. "Any dummy can learn to fight with these. There's always a fifty-fifty chance that you'll lose." "He straightened up and tapped the side of his head. It's harder to learn how to fight with this. If you can... you'll win every time."

"All of that sounds good, but that's not what Gator told me about you. He said you were..." Preach held out his hand to stop him. "I lived it. I don't need to hear it. Which is why I'm telling you that there is another way to make it through the hardship you're facing? I walked a different path. I was broke and in prison. I needed something to eat at night. I would have killed anybody that got in my way back then. Luckily, I didn't have to. Now that God's got me, I don't want the things I don't have. I never needed them. Not food, not money, not even friends. 'He that believes in him is not condemned; but he that does not believe is condemned already, because he has not believed in the name of the only begotten son of God.'"

DeAndre muttered, "John three, eighteen." He smiled at Preach. "I know the word."

"No, you don't. You may have studied the word, but you don't know the word. There's a difference. When you know the word, you have no desire for anything else. You you're searching for acceptance because you don't know what it's like to have a true friend. It's a natural thing."

DeAndre stepped into Preaches cell. He picked up a law book from Preaches bed and sat on the toilet. "I didn't come here to get baptized."

It doesn't matter what you came for. It's what you leave with that's important."

DeAndre thumbed through the law book. The cover read: Federal Horn Book. "I have a problem that God can't fix. Gator is out of control."

"He was never in control," Preach grunted. He showed you the side that he wanted you to see. Now you know the real Gator." DeAndre hung his head low. "Were you doing things for him?"

"He brought guys to play one-on-one." DeAndre couldn't bring himself to tell him about Martin. "I know that he bet on the games, but he never gave me anything."

"And you were a good earner. One that he didn't respect enough to pay. He wouldn't want to let you go."

"Okay, but he's got all kinds of stuff going on."

"What does that matter? Those other hustles; gambling, drugs; all of that comes with risk. With you he got paid without lifting a finger. On top of that, he didn't have to spend to make money. He only had to collect."

None of that was a surprise to DeAndre." How do I get him to leave me alone?"

"He won't. Not yet. You're still valuable."

DeAndre kept turning pages in the law book. Names of cases jumped out at him like; Bounds v. Smith, Taylor v. Starnes, but none of it made sense. He said, "There has to be a way."

"I don't think there's anything that I can tell you. No one can make you do something that you don't want to do. They can try. The decision is yours."

"But you won't teach me to fight?" DeAndre stood up. "If I don't do what he wants, he'll send Keyvon or whoever else at me. I'll have to fight then."

"You might."

A scrap of paper fell out of the book DeAndre was holding. He picked it up. It was an old Polaroid, discolored but clear. "What's this?"

Preach tried to take the picture.

DeAndre jerked it away. He couldn't believe his eyes. The picture showed Preach sitting on the edge of a fountain with a young woman smiling beside him. The young Preach was holding a fat baby in his hands. He looked at Preach with his teeth clenched. "Why do you have a picture of my mother?"

NINE

DeAndre banged his fist against the concrete wall. "Why didn't you tell me?"

Jolene sat still with her mouth ajar, gaze locked on a section of wall just below the dirty glass separating them. "How did you find out?"

"He's here," DeAndre hissed. "Locked up in this hole with me. Twenty-one years. He's been at this prison, right around the corner from us, for nine."

His eyes bore through the thick glass, but she would not look his way.

A shaky hand crept across her forehead. "I thought he would be out of there by now."

"Well, he's not...look at me!" She did, reluctantly. "Why didn't you tell me?"

"Baby, I was going to."

"When? After he was dead, and it would have been too late for me to know? That way you'd never have to face the truth of your dirty little secret."

"DeAndre..."

"DeAndre, what? You're a liar."

Her eyes narrowed to slits, her lips flat. "I understand that you're upset. That's reasonable. But I am a black woman, and I am still your mama. You will not disrespect me. Especially when there is a glass between us, and I can't reach out to pop you upside your damn head."

"I have never disrespected you, but you've got some explaining to do. You can start by telling me why you raised me to believe that my father was dead."

Jolene was quiet for a long time, long enough for her tight mask of frustration to melt into a stretched shadow of sorrow. "A child never knows the sacrifices of a parent until they have children of their own and they have to sacrifice the same."

"That's not an explanation, Mama."

"I've always told you that I grew up without a father."

"He was a deadbeat, nobody told you that he was dead."

She nodded. "Remember when we moved to Raleigh? I bought a house and there was a basketball goal fastened above the garage door."

"I was eleven. I learned to shoot on that goal."

"I know." Jolene smiled at the thought. Her bliss evaporated when she emerged from the daydream, realizing that bouncing ball she heard in her head would never bounce again. "I used to stand in the window watching you. It was the only time you were happy."

"Jolene, we don't have much time left."

She spoke on as if he hadn't interrupted her. "Sometimes you missed a shot and had to chase the ball into the street. No matter how fast the ball bounced away from you, you'd chase it until you had it in your hands. I was so afraid that you would run right into the path of a speeding car." Jolene bit her bottom lip and looked away. "That's what I was trying to save you from."

"What are you talking about?"

"I spent my whole life chasing a dream that my father would someday love me. Before he left, he was my best friend my hero. He took me everywhere that he went. And then...nothing. I blamed myself for his absence as if a five-year-old child had the power to push away a grown man. When my mama yelled to punish me, I cried for my non-existent daddy, wishing he would cascade from the sky like Jesus and whisk me off to some promised land of milk and honey. But that day never came, no matter how hard I cried for it."

"Jolene..."

"No, let me finish. Because, see I always felt incomplete growing up. Like a puzzle missing its most important piece. That may not be important to you, but I can't tell you how much me not being able to let him go, held me back. Only after I pushed those thoughts out of my mind were the chains lifted from my shoulders. I was able to stop focusing on not having his love in order to love myself. The problem I was thirty-two years old." She reached out to touch the glass, running her fingers down its surface as if she was caressing his face. "I told you that your father was dead because I didn't want you chasing a dream of him in the same way that you used to chase that basketball into the street. I didn't want you chasing his ghost like I chased mine. I wanted you to be free to be yourself with nothing holding you back."

DeAndre wanted to say something, but what? She had explained everything and nothing at all, yet it was satisfactory. "I'm sorry that I yelled at you."

A soft smile returned. "Now," she said." Tell me about him. How is he? Okay I hope."

* * *

Preach picked up his rook and killed Percy's bishop.

Percy clapped his hands and yelped; he moved his queen in front of Preaches King. "Checkmate, sucker!"

He surveyed the board. His king had nowhere to move. "Looks like you won again."

They sat on the yard, huddled over the chessboard resting on an overturned five-gallon paint bucket. Officer Leach stood beside the board looking down with his arms folded across his chest. Leach sucked his teeth." Damn, Preach. Stevie Wonder could have seen that trap." Preach sat back in his chair. "I've got a lot on my mind."

Percy pulled out his tally sheet and made a show of whipping it open. "I got something on my mind too. Four-hundred-seventy-eight games to four-twenty-two. I'm catching up."

Leach shook his head. "You couldn't catch up to a turtle in a pickle jar."

"Why you always gotta take his side, Leach?"

"I ain't taking his side, Percy. I'm telling the truth. Y'all been sitting out here playing chess forever. How many of those tally sheets do you have? A hundred? I bet Preach done whupped up on your head."

"Man don't you have a cell to search or something?" Percy asked him. Damn. Always out here harassing folk."

Leach grinned. "I might search your cell, Percy."

"You won't get nothing but practice."

"You need to practice your chess moves." Leach replied.

Percy started setting up the board for a new game. "Whatever, man."

Leach looked to Preach. "What's up with you? You still warmed about that Harris boy?"

"Don't know how I couldn't be."

I don't know what to tell you." Leach stuffed his hands in his pockets. "I've never been apart from my kids. I couldn't imagine meeting my son after twenty-something-odd years." He looked around the enclosed prison yard and sighed. "And in a place like this. Helluva setting for a family reunion."

"What I don't get," Percy said, "Is why she told the boy you were dead? That was cold."

"I don't think she had much choice," Percy explained. "I'm doing life without parole. Got locked up when he was one year old. What was she going to do, bring him to visit me every weekend until the day I die? I know it sounds crazy, but I didn't want my son to grow up seeing me in a cage."

"You told her to leave you alone?" Leach asked. "Damn. Didn't you want to see him? That's your son, man."

"He should 'a had a say in it too, "Percy added. "Y'all took his only chance to know his father. It doesn't matter where you were at. Hell, he might not have ended up in prison if he'd had some fatherly guidance. That's what is wrong with our youth. All the fathers are locked up. Every night you see four or five murders on the news. Twenty-year old kids being sentenced to fifty years in prison. Why?" "Cause there's no one out there raising them."

Preach leaned over with his elbows on his knees. "I don't see how his life could have been any different. If anything, his life turned out better. He didn't have me holding him back."

"How could you hold him back? It takes a man to raise a man."

"I don't know. That's just what I feel that somehow, he was better off without me. I can't answer for God, and I won't try. He set out a plan for my life. Maybe things were just the way they were meant to be."

"What way is that?" A new voice added.

The three men looked to see DeAndre standing behind Leach.

Preach stood.

Leach said, "Guess my break is over. See y'all later." He turned to Percy. "Make sure your cell is straight. I'll be back to shake you down before the day is over."

"Mm-hm," Percy muttered. "I'll leave some dirty drawers on the floor. Skid marks longer than a racing stripe. Just for you." When Leach walked off laughing, Percy started sliding his chess pieces back into their bag. "Guess our game is over."

Preach didn't hear him. He stepped to DeAndre. "I'm glad you came. I didn't know if you wanted to talk to me again, after the way you stormed off yesterday."

"It's not every day that you find out your dead dad is really alive." Preach stood there, not knowing what to say. "Can we walk a little?" DeAndre asked him. "Talk some?"

"Yeah."

They left Percy and walked past a group of men doing push-ups. Two guys were at the end of the yard playing handball.

"Why didn't you tell me sooner?" DeAndre asked. "I've been here for almost a year."

Preach had fought men twice his size and won. He'd battled three or four at a time. He'd always been strong and brave, but never had he been so intimidated that he couldn't meet a man's eyes until now. "I didn't know how to tell you. I didn't know if you would have believed me or thought I was running some kind of game. I figured that I would wait until the right time when you'd be happy to hear it and not reject me."

DeAndre gritted his teeth. "You two are just the same."

"Who are you talking about?"

"I had a visit with my mom a little while ago. We talked about you."

Preach kept walking without saying a word. It was almost like he was living a dream. He had buried that part of his life long ago. He'd always told himself that if a man wanted to survive in prison, he had to let the free world go. That's what he'd done. He didn't just let it go; he threw it away with all the might he could muster. Two decades later it came boomerang back to hit him square in the face.

"She still loves you." DeAndre said.

Preach gawked at him. "She told you that?"

"Nah." DeAndre confessed. "Not in so many words. She'd never admit something like that. But, I've never seen her talk about a man in the way she talked about you. I mean, she dated a few guys, but they never got far. Now that I know, it all makes sense. I think she's been waiting for you to come home all this time."

"I've been gone two decades."

DeAndre rubbed the back of his head. "I don't know how else to explain it."

They walked a few laps in silence, each lost in his own thoughts.

Finally, DeAndre said, "She told me about why you're in prison."

"She never went to my trial. She only knows what she read in the papers."

"She said that you killed a cop. That you were lucky to get life and not the death penalty."

"It's not that simple, DeAndre."

"It never is."

"That cop was my sister's husband. He put his hands on her. She called me crying and begging me to come get her. When I got there, he pulled a pistol on me. I took it from him and tried to walk away.

He came after me. Anything that happened after that wasn't my fault."

DeAndre stared at him. "It really doesn't matter. I know how things can get twisted up in a courtroom. They don't care about what happened. They only use the law to prove their theory of what happened so they can convict you."

"Amen to that, "Preach added.

Gator, Keyvon and Deadman stepped out on the yard as DeAndre and Preach neared the door.

"Schoolboy!" Gator smiled. "Where you been? You ain't came by the crib in a minute." He looked to Preach. "Let me find out you got a new friend." DeAndre didn't reply. "Come on with me. Let's talk. See if we can't heal the wounds our little misunderstanding caused."

DeAndre looked to Preach, who offered no reply. He turned back to Gator. "We don't have anything to talk about."

Gator's smile disappeared. "I ain't asking, Schoolboy."

"And I'm telling you that I don't need to talk to you. I'm good."

Gator's upper lip curled into a snarl. "Deadman."

Deadman didn't hesitate. He charged toward DeAndre with his fists raised and murder in his eyes. Preach stepped in front of his son and pushed DeAndre back. Only then did Deadman give pause.

"Think about what you're doing, son," Preach told him. "Think long and hard."

Deadman swung a wild right. Preach ducked under it and drilled punches from Deadman's lower ribs up to his face. Deadman stumbled back and Preach laid him out with an uppercut.

Keyvon ran up to replace him without being told. Preach remained stooped in a fighting stance. "I haven't done anything to you," he told Keyvon.

Keyvon didn't care. Yet he approached Preach with much more caution than Deadman had. The moved in a tight circle, gauging each other's distance. Keyvon shot a short jab, but not fierce enough to commit. Preach didn't flinch. Keyvon jabbed again. This time Preach slipped it and slide inside close to Keyvon's body. His left hock caught Keyvon in the temple. He was asleep before he hit the concreate.

Preach stepped over the two men and walked toward a backpedaling Gator, who tripped in the bleachers and was forced to sit down.

"You know who I am, "Gator said. "Touch me, and I'll have a hundred soldiers at your door."

Preach stood over him. "Yeah. And when I finish with them, I'll be at yours. I fear no one except God. And, if you try me or my son again, you're going to need Jesus, Jehovah, and Allah to pull me off you."

CHAPTER
TEN

Preach didn't have to see what DeAndre was doing before he looked inside his cell. He'd sharpened enough shanks to recognize the unmistakable scrape of steel grinding against concrete. The worst part of all was that DeAndre had left his cell door unlocked. Anyone could have walked in on him.

Preach yanked open the door without knocking. "It isn't smart to make a shank in the daytime."

DeAndre was sitting cross-legged in the corner of the cell with his back to the door. He jumped out of his skin when he heard the booming voice behind him. The six-inch steel rod he'd been holding clattered to the floor and he fumbled to pick it up.

"Damn, don't sneak up on me like that," DeAndre scolded.

"You're sitting there with your back to the door, and the door wide open. You're asking to be caught."

"I tried to do it at night, but it was taking too long."

Preach peered over his shoulder and saw the long groove DeAndre had worked into the concrete by sliding the tip of the rod against the floor. He shook his head. "It's taking so long because concrete wasn't meant to hone metal. Steel sharpens steel. Dry concrete works against the process because it can be ground away. Use a little water."

DeAndre frowned while staring at the wall. "It doesn't matter. As long as it does the job."

"You're a killer now?"

He started scraping the rod against the floor again. "I'm whatever I have to be to survive. Isn't that what you told me?"

"I did," Preach confessed. "But I didn't have someone like me to guide me down a better path. I did things my way the hard way because I didn't know that waiting on God was an option. "God is the last thing on my mind, right now. It should be the last thing on your mind too." DeAndre spun around to face his father, still sitting. "You think Gator will forget what you did to him?" He couldn't let it go if he wanted to. The yard is talking about how shook you had him. He has to do something."

"I fear no man."

"That's the problem. I do." DeAndre slammed the rod to the floor. "I'm not a fighter. I didn't grow up in the ghetto. Gator knows that. Everybody knows it." He stood up. "I'm not as tough as you, Preach."

"There's a difference between being tough and violent. Tough means dealing with the hardships that come your way and making it through no matter what. It doesn't mean that you have to run around poking holes in people."

DeAndre pushed the hot water button on his sink and wet his right hand. He lathered both with soap by rubbing his hands together furiously. "They're trying to poke me full of holes, or do I have to remind you that they already tried?"

Preach watched him with concerned eyes. "Don't let fear dictate your actions. It will steer you wrong every time. Trust God."

"God! God!" DeAndre threw his hands in the air, spraying soap everywhere. "You're always talking about God. Where was God when my girlfriend was laying in my lap spilling her brains everywhere? Where was God when all those people lied when they testified against me? Huh? I can't pray to a God that won't whisper back when I shout for help. I can't do it."

Preach watched DeAndre's chest heave with fists tight at his sides. He knew what it felt like to call out to God and get no response or to think that he had gotten no response. Maturity taught him that those moments of supposed silence were a test of faith. Sometimes he failed and learned how easy it was to give in to negative temptation. The true challenge was living up to his potential as a responsible man.

Preach had questioned God often, asking why he had to live and die in a cell when so many others had done worse and were punished less. He couldn't understand, and as the years passed, he realized that the will of God was not for him to understand, but to deal with whatever was set out before him in the best way that he could. He accepted the fact that his earthly reward may not come in the form of freedom, but that he could obtain riches with peace of mind.

His soul burned to express this logic to DeAndre, but the young man wasn't ready. Preach was his father, but the boy never had a Dad. Those long afternoons tossing around the pigskin in the backyard were fantasies that would never be fulfilled. He reasoned that it wasn't appropriate to try to be a father so late in the game. The best he could hope for was that DeAndre allowed him to be a friend.

"I cried out to God too," Preach said. "For a long time, nothing happened. But when you showed up, and I was able to lay eyes on you, I knew that God had heard every word. My problem was patience."

DeAndre didn't give an immediate response. His breathing slowed. His muscles relented. He reached over and grabbed a towel off his bed to dry his hands.

Preach looked at the short steel rod laying on the floor. He held out his hand. "Let me get that knife."

DeAndre stared at Preaches open palm, then met his eyes. "You're saying that I should wait? Wait for what?"

The answer came easily to Preach. "A better way."

DeAndre picked up the shank and handed it to Preach.

Preach left the cell, walked to a trashcan and threw it away. When he went back to DeAndre's cell, DeAndre was sitting on the edge of his bunk with his face buried in his hands.

Preach leaned against the door frame. "God answered another prayer."

DeAndre was silently debating as to whether giving up his knife had been a mistake. "Yeah? What was that?"

"I asked him to make sure that your mother raised you right."

DeAndre gestured to the cell enclosing him in. "I still ended up here."

"It's not a reflection of her. I had a good mama too."

"If she was such a good woman, why did you leave her?"

Preach slid down to a crouch. "I can't say that I left. Things weren't working out. Your mother needed a man to be as good as she was a good woman. That wasn't me."

"Preach...you're saying a lot, but you aren't saying anything at all."

"I guess I owe you an explanation."

"You don't owe me anything, but I'd like to know."

Preach rubbed his eyes. "I was raised in Raleigh, southeast Raleigh. My mama drove a city bus. My father was a ghost. I was raised in the streets. By sixteen most of my friends had already done a prison bid or been shot. I wanted more. I went into the Navy the day after graduation.

"After basic training they sent me to the Great Lakes Training facility, near Waukegan, IL. On a leave some buddies and me went to Chicago to see the city and hang out. Your mother was working at a shoe store on Michigan Avenue."

Preach stared off into space, smiling at the memory." I don't believe in love at first site, but I knew that I would marry her the first time our eyes met." He glanced to DeAndre. "You ever felt like that?"

DeAndre shook his head. "No."

Preach slumped at that revelation. "I hope you will someday." He paused, remember catching his reflection in a picture window on Michigan Avenue. He'd been slim and trim, clean in his bleached white uniform. Jolene snuggled close, standing on tip toes to kiss him. "We never married, but once I got out of the military, she moved to North Carolina with me. I loved her, but I was young and not ready to be in a permanent relationship."

"You cheated on her?"

"Nah. It wasn't like that. I couldn't handle the responsibility. I drank a lot. I mean, I'd been in the Navy. We weren't on a boat, we were drunk. It was hard to change that. We argued all the time. There were days when I didn't want to go home after work because we were beefing so hard."

DeAndre smirked. "Let me guess. It got worse when I was born."

"Not really. I had the whole nine months that she was pregnant to get right. And after you were born, things were okay at first. But over time, the arguing started again. This time we didn't argue about drinking. It was everything else.

"She moved back to Chicago a month after you were born. When she left, I got worse. I knew that her taking you away was all my fault. I had all of this pent-up rage inside that I didn't know what to do with. When my sister called and asked me to pick her up because my brother-in-law had hit her, I found a target to unleash my frustrations."

DeAndre was quiet while he thought about that. His life had been ruined because his parents couldn't get along. A child raised in an imbalanced home can only grow to be imbalanced and incomplete. He wondered how his life would have turned out if Preach had found his way sooner...but strangely, he wasn't upset. Their breaking up hadn't been about him. As a man, he understood that.

He asked Preach, "When was the last time you spoke to her?"

"The day that she left for Chicago. Over two decades ago."

"Why didn't you call her?"

Preach stood up. "Call her? What? I can't—I couldn't..."

"You want to apologize, right?"

"Look, I know what you're trying to do, but..."

DeAndre stepped to him. "All I'm trying to do is help y'all get on the same page. You don't have to be together to be friends. I think she'd like to hear from you."

***

DeAndre waited until his mother accepted the phone call, then he handed the phone to Preach. The older man stood there, looking at DeAndre, who mouthed the word "talk," then walked away.

Preach stared at the phone in his hand. He smiled while raising it to his ear. "Jolene?"

A pregnant pause. "David? Where's DeAndre? Tell me that my boy is okay. I wouldn't be able to live if…"

"He's fine, Jolene. He-uh-he said that I should call you."

Her words were shaky on the other end. "Okay. How…how are you?"

"I'm great." The sound of her made his heart quicken. "Listen. It's been a long time. I've owed you an apology for twenty-odd years."

"Oh, David. I don't need any apology."

"You do. I should have been a better man. You were the best woman that I could have asked for. If I'd done what I was supposed to do, we would still be together right now. So, I'm sorry."

The phone went silent for a long time. He heard children playing in the background. The scream of an airplane in the distance. He guessed that she must have been outside or parked so that she could talk to him.

"David. Thank you, but I owe you an apology too. I expected too much of you. You had your boxing and your friends. I didn't think you had enough time for me. I was selfish."

"We were young." He said.

"We were."

"Maybe we can start over. As friends."

"I'd like that." A comfortable silence commandeered the phone until Jolene asked, "How is DeAndre making it?"

Preach let a moment dangle while deciding on whether to tell her the truth or not. "He's not used to this life. He had a different path set out before him. Prison wasn't it."

"But you've been helping him, right?"

"I'm doing all I can do. He's my son too. Jolene, I'd die for him if it came to that."

She sighed. "I hope it doesn't. Lord knows he doesn't deserve to suffer in there."

"I haven't asked him about his case yet. All I know is what I read in the paper."

"He's innocent. David."

"Have you thought about getting him a lawyer? It's not cheap, but he might see some light."

"I don't have the money. Not now."

"If you don't like him being here, something has to be done."

"What about in there. Can't he do it himself?"

Preach winced. "Not really. The state doesn't allow us to have a law library. I've helped some people, but with a lawyer, he'd have a better chance."

"A lawyer isn't an option right now. Is there a way that you can help him?"

Preach thought about it. "I don't want to screw it up. He's only got one good shot at an appeal. If it doesn't work…"

"David, can you help him?"

"I can try."

"Please do."

Preach slid on a pair of thick black rimmed reading glasses and stared down at the pile of papers on the table before him like an overstuffed man at a buffet. He blew out hard. "Been a long time since I did this."

He picked up the first document on top of the stock. The indictment. He read every sentence at least three times, then he put that down and read DeAndre's judgement and commitment papers. Preach tip toed through each document meticulously, even looking for misspellings and erroneous punctuation.

DeAndre sat watching in silence for thirty minutes. "Shouldn't you go through my trial transcripts first? Isn't that where the important stuff is?"

"Everything is important. The only way a prisoner can get a new trial is through constitutional violations. You have to show the court that your rights have been violated."

"Okay." What about lying witnesses? Those are in the transcripts."

Preach took off his glasses and placed them on the table. "Most people don't get help because somebody lied on them. Even if it happened, you have to prove it. That could take new evidence and sworn affidavits supporting your claims. On the flip side I've seen guys with life sentences get out because the clerk of court didn't have a copy of one specific document. I knew another one who got sixty years knocked off because all the elements of the crime he was charged with weren't listed in the indictment. When your life is concerned, every detail is important. I get it you're bored, but I need you to pay attention to this stuff, okay."

DeAndre felt like a six-year-old child getting in the way of his father's work. He quickly disappeared from Preaches focus and sat there as the invisible man for fifteen more minutes. His old man didn't notice when he got up and went to his cell. He wanted to help in some way, but his ignorance of the law would only hinder Preaches progress.

Time was of the essence.

Preach had explained that the federal courts only allowed habeas corpus appeals within one year after the denial of his last state appeal. It was an unfair rule, and DeAndre didn't have much time left. A few months at the most. That was no time for on-the-job training. It was best to let Preach work.

After some time, Preach brought the papers back to DeAndre's cell. "I've been through these. Keep them separate. I'll start on the transcripts tomorrow." He pointed to the papers he'd handed to DeAndre. "You should look through them too. You know your case better than anybody else. You might find something I missed. If you're not sure about something, ask me."

Later they ate dinner, then went to the yard around five o'clock. Preach took daily walks, and today DeAndre strolled with him.

They had become close over the past few weeks. The heat DeAndre felt from Gator and his goons had died down, just like Preach said it would. DeAndre didn't feel safe, but he wasn't tiptoeing around the prison either.

"Do you think I have a chance to get out?" DeAndre asked.

"I don't know yet."

Though their relationship had grown, DeAndre had never spoken about his crime, and Preach had never asked. Even though they were family, they were still convicts.

DeAndre took a deep breath. "I'm in prison for something I didn't do."

"Innocence won't get you out of prison. It never does. Disproving the state's evidence against you is your only path to freedom."

The afternoon sun was still high and warm. They walked past old men playing shuffleboard. DeAndre had heard that one of the players, Doc McCoy, was eighty-three and had been in prison for fifty years. DeAndre couldn't imagine being in prison for such a long time. Death seemed like a better alternative.

"Look around you," Preach told him. "Prisons are chuck full of people who have lost the fire to fight. They lost hope, because someone explained the same things, I'm telling you, and they quit. Decades later they're sitting in this yard wondering if they could have righted the wrongs done to them. Do you want that to be you?"

DeAndre stared at Doc McCoy and hunched over and struggling to slide a disk with a long wooden stick. "No, "he said, I don't"

"Okay then. You need to think about the things I say and give me any kind of information that could help you."

It had been a long time since the incident. So long that DeAndre thought the hurt he'd felt from the conviction had dissipated. He was wrong. The truth was that he hadn't thought about it. He'd pushed it to the back of his mind and pretended that the pain didn't exist as a way to cope with it.

He wasn't sure if he could talk about it. He had never told anyone about what happened that night.

"DeAndre," Preach said. "What happened?"

He wasn't sure where to begin, so he just started talking. "We had a short team meeting after the NCAA Championship. I was tired. I just wanted to go home. Everyone was talking about going to a celebration party. I didn't want to go, but Michael told me I had to go because we would not have won without me."

"Who's Michael?"

"You don't know who Michael Artiste is?"

Preach thought about it. "Are you talking about the guy that just signed a huge contract with, uh some NBA team?"

"Yeah, him. We were like Jordan and Pippen on the court. Unstoppable."

"You went to the party with him?"

DeAndre nodded. "Tabitha wanted to go too, but her roommate had to work, so we swung by and picked her up."

"Tabitha was your girlfriend? The one that died?" DeAndre nodded again. "Michael was driving?"

DeAndre went silent. He felt his blood run hot in his veins. "He was my best friend, or, at least I thought he was."

Exhuming the skeletons of the past helped him to see clearer in hindsight than he had back then. He realized that he and Michael always had a love/hate rivalry that only talented teammates can have. There were times when he'd be competing more against Michael on the court than the other team. He set a scoring record of sixty-five points in one game by trying to outscore Michael. Their relationship never seemed toxic until now.

"We argued on the way to the party. He was mad that I took the last shot when I could have passed it to him."

"But y'all won? And he was still mad?"

"Messed me up too. If he had taken the last shot, and we lost, I would have been cool with it. We were a team. But he wouldn't let it go."

Preach listened quietly for a time. Then he asked, "Which one of you had the gun?"

DeAndre looked at him. "How did you know one of us had a gun?"

"I didn't until you gave me that stupid look. So, was it your or him?"

"We got to the party..."

***

It was the biggest party that DeAndre had ever been to. He saw his jersey everywhere that he looked, #27. He was actually afraid to get out and be moved by the crowd after Michael parked. Tabitha kissed him and hopped out of the backseat to meet her friends standing on the lawn.

Michael and DeAndre sat in the car watching the massive crowd.

"All those people... here to see you, my dude," Michael said. "Hero for today."

DeAndre noted the acid singing Michael's words. "I took the shot, Michael, and I made it. Let it go. Enjoy the moment."

"You're always taking the shot. Always a leg up on me. You'll probably go in the first round of the draft."

"I don't care. As long as I get drafted."

Michael turned in his seat. "See that's the difference between you and me. Being on top of the world doesn't matter to you. It does to me. I want to be the best."

DeAndre could tell that this thing kept Michael up late at night, anxiety knotting his belly as he thought about someone performing better than him and stealing his shine. "I just try to put the ball in the hoop, DeAndre admitted. His non-Challans drew a tight grimace from Michael.

"Michael…" "We've got a party to go to. Look under your seat and hand me that."

DeAndre reached beneath his seat. "That" turned out to be a Barretta nine-millimeter. Before handing it over, DeAndre held it with his finger tensed on the trigger.

Michael snatched the gun. "Be careful with that. It's loaded." He stuffed the gun into his waistband at the crotch.

DeAndre watched him blouse his shirt over the bulge. "What do you need that for? It's a good night. Everybody's cooling. There shouldn't be any drama."

"You don't come from where I come from, D."

"What does that have to do with anything?"

"I was born and raised in Compton. Dudes was shooting at baby showers. You gotta be on point at all times. Many people love you for what you did tonight, and a lot of people hate you too. It's going to be hard to tell which is which. That's why I stay ready. I don't trust nobody."

DeAndre glared at him. "Don't you trust me?"

Michael got out of the car without a response.

DeAndre followed and was immediately accosted by Tabitha, who stuck her arm around his waist. "You okay, baby?" He asked her.

"No. There are a million FANS out here waiting for you to show your face. As far as I'm concerned, we're Siamese twins joined at the hips for the night."

DeAndre laughed, knowing how serious she was. They'd been talking marriage lately. DeAndre wanted to wait until after he'd landed a contract with an NBA team. That way their first house could be a mansion. He wanted to give her the best.

They entered the house. Five kegs of beer were lined up in the center of the kitchen. A female was held upside down while guzzling beer from a tube in a keg stand. A small crowd around her chanted, "Drink! Drink! Drink!"

DeAndre couldn't take one more step without four people telling him about how wonderful he was. A lesser man may have swelled with pride at such a display. To DeAndre it was annoying. He'd never set out to be anyone's hero, and he didn't enjoy being treated as one.

He saw Michael break away and weave through the crowd toward a few guys on their team standing in a corner of the living room.

"What's wrong with him?" Tabitha asked. "He's been acting moody all night."

DeAndre pulled her closer. "He'll get over it."

He and Tabitha were headed toward a patio at the back of the house when some guy bumped DeAndre's shoulder. The bump was way too forceful to have been an accident. "Watch where you're going!" The guy said.

DeAndre glared at him but didn't respond. He turned and kept walking.

The guy grabbed DeAndre's arm and spun him around. "Did you hear me talking to you?"

Through the crowd, DeAndre saw Michael moving toward them with a purpose. A few of their teammates were behind him.

"It was an accident," DeAndre told him.

"I know who you are. I don't care about what a star you are on the court." He pushed DeAndre in the chest.

"Don't put your hands on me."

He pushed DeAndre again.

DeAndre drew back and hit him. He wasn't trying to fight. It was more of a reflex than anything else. After that, all he remembered was being caught up in a whirlwind of pumping fists, twisting bodies, and pain.

He wasn't thinking. That's how Tabitha got caught up in the whole thing. He had forgotten that she was beside him until he heard her scream. Then the fight became less about pride, and more about getting her out of there.

Michael was getting beaten pretty badly. He was fighting two guys at once. DeAndre saw him reach for the pistol as if it were slow motion, or an instant replay. He aimed at one of his assailants. The guy slapped the pistol away so that the barrel pointed straight at DeAndre's face. He hit the floor just as the gun went off.

One gunshot. That's all it had taken. The surrounding crowd stampeded toward every visible exit, searching for safety.

Everyone except Tabitha.

Preach walked with his eyes looking down at the concrete as he listened.

"The police testified that my fingerprints were on the gun."

"Because you picked it up while you were in the car." Preach said. "Sad story."

DeAndre looked up at the sky. The blue that it once was had faded to a glowing orange as the sun began its descent over the edge of the earth. Tabitha was there somewhere, looking down on him.

Preach brought him back to reality. "Did you ever tell the police it was Michael's gun, or that he shot your girlfriend?" DeAndre shook his head. "Why not? You wouldn't be here now if you had." "I didn't want to snitch on him. And I didn't think they would try to pin it on me."

"The police would blame a ham sandwich for a murder if they could get away with it. Did they test your hands or clothes for gunpowder residue, to see if you had fired a gun?"

"No."

Preach grit his teeth. "Was Michael ever a suspect?"

"They questioned him before talking to me. He denied everything. They asked him if he'd seen me with a gun, and he told them he had. Not that night, but before."

"Is that statement in your paperwork?"

"It's in my Motion of Discovery, you know, all the evidence that the state had against me."

"Did he testify at your trial?"

DeAndre sighed, hating to relive those moments." He testified that I brought a gun to the party, and that he saw me fire into the crowd." Preach groaned but said nothing.

"Do you think I have a chance to prove that he was lying? No one else said that about me. They all knew who I was, but they said they weren't sure who was shooting."

"I don't know. It won't be easy. Since he testified to something different from what he said to police at first, shows an inconsistency, but the courts need more than that. We will need current case law."

"How do we get that? The State doesn't give us access to a law library."

"We'll have to find someone to print it off the interned. And we need it fast."

***

Officer Martin knocked on DeAndre's door as soon as she began her shift the next morning. "Wake up, sleepyhead," she said after opening his cell door.

DeAndre sat up. "Melody. I-uh-I've got a favor to ask you."

Officer Martin was working DeAndre's housing floor the next day. He walked out into the lobby as she was hunched over the desk doing paperwork. The sight of her made his heart quicken. She was gorgeous. Had her natural hair pulled back into a poof at the back of her head. Her lips were freshly glossed and looked like two succulent pieces of fruit.

She put her pen down and smiled as he approached. "Will you help me get something out of the utility closet?" she stood and reached for the large ring of brass keys dangling from her pant loop. "I'm out of toilet paper."

The utility closed was behind a locked door to the left of the lobby. It was really a small room where an abundance of toilet paper, cleaning supplies, soap and writing paper were stored for the inmate population.

DeAndre stared into the rectangular window sitting at eye level in the door. With the lights out inside of the closed, you could see only your reflection from the outside.

She unlocked the door. DeAndre flipped on the light switch as he entered. Martin closed the door behind them. A manila envelope, bulging with papers, sat on top of an over-sized toilet paper box. DeAndre picked it up and peeked inside. There were ten or so printed legal cases inside.

Martin stood just inside the doorway, watching him. "That's most of them from the list you gave me. I have five more to bring, but the envelop was too small for them all."

"It's okay." DeAndre smiled. "I'm happy to have any at all."

DeAndre sat the envelope down and picked up a large trash bag. He shook it open and started stuffing it full of fresh rolls of toilet paper. Martin slowly walked over to him.

"I can't thank you enough," he continued. "You do not understand how hard it is to get legal materials in here. Damn near impossible."

Martin reached down and touched his wrist to stop him from moving. "I'll do anything for you, DeAndre. You know that. There's no need to thank me."

He stood to face her. "But, Melody. You take a risk of getting fired by slipping me a stick of chewing gum. I know when somebody is standing on a limb for me."

Her hands slid up and down his forearms. "It doesn't matter. Whatever you need or want is yours. All you have to do is ask me." She inched closer, so close that their lips were almost touching. "I want you out of here. You don't belong in a place like this."

Martin's hands on his arms raised goosebumps all over his body. "Melody…"

Her palms moved to his obliques. Fingernails dug into his sides as she pulled him into a long kiss.

Fear froze him still. His eyes were wide open and staring out of the window looking into the lobby. He wasn't afraid of going to the hole. He had accepted that fate as a fact of prison life. He was concerned about what could happen to Martin if they got caught.

He'd seen quite a few women fired for dealing with inmates in his short time as a prisoner. The most memorable was a pretty, red-headed nurse who was handcuffed and paraded down a long hallway call 'The Tunnel' for all to see. "I need this job"," She'd said, tears staining her face. "I have to care for my kids." But none of that mattered to prison officials who wanted to make a point.

The message was clear; This is what happens when you mess with inmates.

Her lips were magnets though, drawing him in. Butterflies in his belly fluttered away as he gave in to her passion. His fear did not fade away, but her abandonment pushed him closer to fear-less-ness.

"Wait!" She said after pulling away.

His lips chased hers. "Wait?" Just when he was getting into it.

Martin moved close to the door and peered out of the small window. Satisfied that no one had seen them go, not the closed, she flipped the switch down, bathing the room in darkness. The only light was an elongated checker beaming in the center of the floor.

It was so dark that he didn't see her move. He felt her hands, soft at first, flat against his chest. She then shoved him into the wall, DeAndre wrapped his arms around her waist to pull her closer. She fit perfectly in his grip.

A long time had passed since he held a woman. In some ways, he thought he would never hold a woman again. The sensation was foreign, but he got used to it.

And then she was tugging the tail of his t-shirt out of his pants. Her hands slipped beneath the garment and slid against his warm flesh as she kissed him. Her fingernails, raking his skin, sent chills up his spine.

In turn, his hands slunk below her belt to cup her behind and pull her closer.

"If we're going to do this... we need to hurry," she whispered.

He buried his lips in the crook of her neck and planted kisses north to the soft spot behind her ear. "Are you sure you want to go that far?" He asked.

She answered him with a deep kiss, more passionate than all the kisses before it. Her hands traveled lower and yanked his belt open.

Just as her fingers wedge into his waistband, her walkie-talkie squawked, echoing in the small room, startling them. "Sargent Johns to Officer Martin, over."

Martin froze. It took her a moment to realize that the communication was for her. She snatched the radio from her hip and lifted it to her mouth. "Go for Martin."

What's your twenty?"

"WRB. Second floor," she replied.

"Give me a twenty-nine at extension two-two-seven."

"Ten-four." She lowered the radio. "Damn," she hissed. "He wants me to call him. Perfect timing. "She caressed his neck. "I'm sorry, baby."

DeAndre leaned against the wall, grinning in the darkness. "Sorry for what? I was lucky to have you for the small time that I could."

She leaned in to kiss him again.

He allowed it for a while, but he had to push her away. "Go handle your business."

"I will."

Martin left.

DeAndre finished loading the trash bag full of toilet paper with a smile on his face.

***

The next few weeks flew by in a blur. DeAndre and Preach studied the first round of cases, which led to another list, and another, all of which Martin was happy to provide.

"I'll do anything that will bring you closer to me." She told DeAndre. "I've got a bubble bath waiting with your name on it."

DeAndre discovered that studying legal cases was a lot like doing research for a term paper. He scribbled lists of relevant information and analyzed them to determine what was the most important.

At first, Preach was skeptical about DeAndre helping him. Legal work took patience and a meticulous method that most people weren't suited for. As time went on, Preach saw that DeAndre's competitive spirit was easily shifted to legal work. Where a lot of men would have become frustrated and given up, DeAndre pressed harder. Preach learned to welcome the help.

Six weeks later, Martin showed up at his cell and handed him the last manila envelope. Inside were three typed copies of DeAndre's Motion for Appropriate Relief, ready to be signed and sent to the Wake County Superior Court.

DeAndre took the package and held it as if it was the key to the front door of the prison. "Thank you for typing this, Melody. None of this would have been possible without you."

She smiled. I'm not a lawyer, but it was very well written. You guys did a good job."

"I don't know if it will get me out of here."

"DeAndre, you did the best that you could have done. It will count for something."

DeAndre took the package to Preaches cell. The old man read the motion and nodded approvingly when he finished. "I didn't find one typo."

"Yeah, she did great."

Preach handed it back to him. "Get it notarized and in the mailbox."

"I hope we can win, "DeAndre said, staring at the motion, not believing that they had done it and he had a chance to be heard on his terms.

"I hope so, too. But you have to remember that your chances of getting a new trial are slim. Judges don't like it when a prisoner proves the state wrong. If you get turned down this first time, it doesn't mean that you can't win later on down the road."

DeAndre listened, but he wouldn't let his hope be dashed. "We'll win. I feel it."

***

DeAndre floated on a cloud of triumph all that day.

He entered the gym with plans to get in a good workout. It was a bright day. Sidewinder, Chino, and Danny were playing a pickup game of twenty-one. None of them was very good. Danny was quick, but he lacked precision when he released the ball for a jump shot. Chino was clumsy and all over the place. Sidewinder had good shooting form but hobbled on a crippled hip that wouldn't allow him to run as fast as he wanted to.

He watched them for a while, thinking he'd never seen three worse ballers.

To his right, the recreation coordinator sat at a folding table. A bunch of cons were crowded around it, reading something. DeAndre walked over. They were looking at a sign-up sheet for the prison's summer basketball tournament. One man signed his name to a team roster. Another was quick to grab the pen next and do the same.

DeAndre was turning away when he bumped into Gator.

"Schoolboy!" Gator put on his brightest smile. "It's been awhile."

DeAndre took a step back. "Not long enough."

Gator draped his arm across DeAndre's shoulders. "There's a lot of money riding on this tournament."

"That's only if you're betting. I'm not."

"I am. It'd be a shame to see some suckers win this thing. Especially when you could be the star of the show."

"I'm good," DeAndre told him.

"You ain't good until you play for my team."

DeAndre shrugged. "I can't."

"Why not?"

"I'm already on a team."

Gator scanned the team rosters on the table. "I don't see your name."

DeAndre took the ink pen and scribbled in his name. "There it is."

Gator chuckled. "You are playing by yourself?"

DeAndre stared at the blank spaces beneath his name. He turned to the court, drawn to the sound of a dribbling basketball. He watched Chino go up for a lay-up. He missed, but he laughed when he hit the ground. DeAndre smiled at the sight, pleased to see someone enjoy the game for what it was, a game.

He wrote down three names below his own.

THIRTEEN

"You're short one player." Preach said after DeAndre told him about what he'd done.

He and Preach stood on the side-lines of the last basketball court watching as Chino, Sidewinder, and Danny came walking toward them. Chino was the shortest of the trio at five' nine. Danny was six' one and built with lean muscle. Sidewinder was average height and slim, but he walked with a winding twist in his left hip because of an injury he'd suffered as a child.

Preach crossed his arm. "That's the squad you want to run with?"

"Yup." DeAndre shuffled a basketball from hand to hand.

"Looks like you've got a lot of work cut out for you."

DeAndre smiled. "Kinda."

"What does that mean?"

"I'm not trying to win, Preach. I didn't want to play for Gator."

Preach thought about that. "Why didn't you just say no? No man can force you to do something you don't want to do."

"It wasn't that sample."

"It was. Look, I know you don't want a confrontation with Gator, but you can't let it dictate your manhood. If you don't want to do something, speak your mind and deal with whatever comes after."

"You're right," DeAndre told him. "I'll do it next time."

"You should have done it this time. Because you've got three guys on your team that don't know you aren't planning to win."

The trio of DeAndre's team was almost upon them. With the vail of DeAndre's intention to lose lifted, he saw the men for what they were; a group of scrubs that had no chance to win. Preach turned and started walking away.

"Where are you going? DeAndre asked him.

"To play chess."

"Aren't you going to help me coach?"

Preach kept walking. "I play to win. Not to lose."

Chino held out his hands for DeAndre to pass him the ball as he neared.

DeAndre wouldn't pass it to him. "No ball handling right now. Gotta stretch first."

"Stretch?" Chino scoffed. "What is this, ballet? I don't need to stretch."

"You do. Stretching reduces your chances of injury. The better you stretch, the better your performance on the court." DeAndre had always been serious about stretching. He'd taken yoga classes while in high school at the advice of his coach and went through a battery of strenuous poses before each game. His goal wasn't just to prolong his health, but to gain any edge that he could over his opponents. Flexibility meant that he could push his body harder, stay on the court longer, and stay energetic while his opponents tired out.

That was the obsession of his competitiveness. He'd never thought he would be a great player just by shooting jump-shots. He spent more time strengthening the muscles that propelled the ball versus trying to put the ball in the hoop. That work ethic set him aside from players that were naturally gifted.

DeAndre lined them up shoulder to shoulder and stood in front of them. He began with easy standing arm stretches and shoulder rotations. After that he moved to the trunk, leading them through light bends to loosen the torso and get some movement in their spines. Finally, they sank into a long series of leg stretches.

He noticed that Chino kept staring at a group of men pumping weights on a bench press. The guys lifting shot frowns at DeAndre and his team stretching.

"Don't worry about them, Chino," DeAndre said.

"Why can't we lift weights like them?"

He saw that both China and Sidewinder had puddles of sweat beneath them. That meant that the stretching was working, and that they were in pain.

DeAndre kept them in a wide leg stretch. "Lifting weights without stretching will make you move like a robot on the court."

Sidewinder's whole body trembled. "How much longer do we have to go?"

"Not much longer, "DeAndre told him.

Sidewinder couldn't take it. He inched up to a standing position. "I can't take any more. Hurts too bad."

Chino stood too.

"The pain won't last," DeAndre told them. "Look at Danny. He can handle it."

Danny's legs were stretched out wider than DeAndre's, almost into a full split. He looked calm and comfortable.

"He stretches all the time," Chino complained.

After the stretch, DeAndre took them on a mile run. Everybody made it, even Sidewinder, who limped for the last three laps.

DeAndre gathered them, sweaty and heaving beneath one basketball goal. "I know you guys play ball, but have any of you ever played under the whistle?"

Nobody raised their hand.

"In street ball," he continued. "hard fouls are allowed. Under a whistle, every touch counts either as a foul or a potential point. Our goal is to turn every touch into a point, even when the other team is fouling the hell out of you."

He taught them some passing drills, really to gauge their abilities. Once he was sure that they could pass well, he gave them the ball to get a game of twenty-one going for fun. Everyone wanted to play. No one wanted to practice. It was a fact of human nature. But what they took for fun, DeAndre used to further scout their talents.

Sidewinder was slow. He could move well laterally, but he couldn't cut after running forward.

Chino was quick like a cat. He wasn't the best dribbler, but he could hold on to the ball and was consistent with his shots, whether beneath the basket or at a long range.

Preach ambled over and stood beside DeAndre. "How did you get Daniels to play?"

"Daniels?"

Preach pointed. "The tall guy they call Danny."

DeAndre shrugged. "He kinda came with them. He doesn't talk much. Hasn't said one word all day. Some people say he's a lunatic."

"People say a lot of things. I was with him at Broutal Correctional. He's not crazy. Just quiet. The guy was locked up since he was twelve or thirteen. I heard that they overturned his life sentence because he was a juvenile when he was convicted. If that's true, he'll make parole in a few years."

"What about Chino?"

"Foolish. Always in some trouble. Typical young kid."

"Sidewinder?"

A follower. Dope fiend. I think he could straighten up if he had a role model. Sometimes that's all a misguided man needs, you know, someone to steer him right."

They stood watching in silence for a time. Chino shot the ball. It bounced off the rim. Danny rebounded, dribbled to the three-point line and drilled the shot."

"He can shoot," Preach said.

"Yeah. Good arch. Accurate."

Preach smirked. "You'd know better than me."

They heard snickering laughter down by the exit door. DeAndre looked and saw Keyvon and three other guys pointing and laughing at DeAndre's team. They were too far away for DeAndre to hear exactly what they said, but he was well aware that Keyvon wanted his laughter to be heard. DeAndre noticed that his team had stopped playing. He told Chino to take a shot.

"What?"

"Take a shot!"

Chino looked at the laughing men, then turned toward the basket and shot a low arching three-pointer.

DeAndre took off running and hopped to catch the ball mid-air. He swooped it between his legs and slammed it down with the force of a freight train smashing into a brick wall. He said nothing when he landed, just looked down at Keyvon and the others who were no longer laughing.

Preach started clapping.

DeAndre looked at his team. "We're done for today. Good job."

***

They practiced every day after breakfast and lunch. Other teams practiced, but none of them went at it as relentlessly as DeAndre's team. They ran miles, sprinted suicides, and did backboard-tap drills until they couldn't jump anymore.

It was during those times when they were dogged tired and dripping sweat that DeAndre taught them the real secrets of the game.

He dribbled to the top of the key and told Chino to guard him. DeAndre dribbled the ball from hand to hand. "Okay. Good. Stay low, just like that. Keep your hands wide. You watching Danny?" DeAndre faked left. When Chino followed in that direction, DeAndre dribbled the ball back to his right hand and jerked Chino's wrist to his left as he went right. DeAndre was leaping in the air and dunking by the time Chino realized what had happened.

"You can't do that," Chino protested.

DeAndre walked toward him. "Do what?"

"You yanked my wrist. That was dirty, dog"

DeAndre looked to Danny. "Danny, you were standing about where a referee would have been. Did you see me do anything wrong? Any fouls?"

Danny shook his head.

"See," DeAndre continued. "That's what I was talking about. You have to turn a foul into a point. Now, Chino, come here." He gave Chino the ball and taught him how to do it. Chino nailed it on the first try. "It happens so quick that most people will miss it, unless they know to look for it."

Sidewinder was amazed. "Yo. Where d'you learn that?"

"Michael Jordan basketball camp."

Chino's eyes bulged. "You met Michael Jordan?"

DeAndre shrugged. "He only came one day out of three. All I saw was the back of his head." He positioned Chino in front of Danny. "Chino, you go, then give Danny a turn. After that, teach sidewinder."

He stepped off to the sidelines. The group of misfits he'd assembled were beginning to show potential, where before there was none. No one wanted these guys on their team during quick games. They were the scrubs who played on the small courts while the big boys played on the main one. Now, the alpha males stood on the sidelines watching DeAndre's team practice, respect in their eyes.

Preach stepped to DeAndre. They watched Chino instruct Sidewinder. "Looks like you had a change in mission."

"What do you mean?"

"Before you said that, the only reason you chose a team was because you didn't want to play for Gator. Now it looks like you're playing to win."

"DeAndre flashed a half smile. "Yeah. Looks that way, doesn't it?"

FOURTEEN

It was high noon when the group of four moseyed down to the court where DeAndre and his team were practicing. Three fit black guys and one tall white prisoner that they all called Ice.

Ice walked up on DeAndre. "Y'all been on this court all morning. We want to play ball too."

Chino slapped the ball in his hands to draw the attention to himself. "It's called practice, bro. Go get on one of the other courts. If you ask real nice, I'm sure they'll let you play."

One of Ice's friends, Choppy, pointed at Chino. "You've got a big mouth."

"Yup. Big enough to take a chunk out of your ass."

DeAndre held up his hand to silence Chino. He said, "Look. We don't have a problem giving you the court, but we want to play too. If you want this court so bad, why don't you take it from us?"

Ice threw up his fists. "I ain't never been scared of a fight."

DeAndre took the ball from Chino. "I'm not talking about fighting." He bounced the ball to Ice. "Check ball."

Ice caught the ball and smiled. He took a look at DeAndre's squad with amusement in his eyes. "You serious?" Choppy and his friends started taking off their shirts.

DeAndre gathered his team in a huddle.

Sidewinder peeked at the other team. Two of them were tight, muscular physiques. He raised his eyebrows. "You sure we're ready for this?"

DeAndre shook his head. "No, but it doesn't matter. All you have to do is play your game and do what I taught you to.

Ice posted up at the free throw line. He had a slim, swimmer's body with the handle of an automatic pistol tattooed on his belly as if he had a pistol stuffed in his pants. "We gonna play, or what?"

DeAndre faced him. "Make it take it?" Ice thought about it, then nodded. DeAndre asked, "What are we playing to?"

"Ten. And after we whup you, y'all can get off my court."

Ice and DeAndre shot three rounds of free-throws to determine who got first possession. Ice missed his third shot, so DeAndre took the ball out. His guys spread out like he taught them to. He inbounded to Chino.

"Take your time," DeAndre called out as he trotted to get open.

Choppy hustled to guard Chino. He pressed Chino hard so that Chino couldn't gain any ground on him. Frustrated, Chino passed the ball to DeAndre. DeAndre passed the ball to Sidewinder as soon as it his hands. Sidewinder popped a weak shot that bounced off the front of the rim. Ice quickly rebounded. He passed the ball around. Choppy launched a shot from the inner left of the court and made it.

Ice took the ball out. DeAndre hurried to D-up.

Ice passed to a teammate who passed it right back. "I used to watch you play on TV." Ice told DeAndre as he backed him down. "I used to think you were the next Jordan. But now that I'm playing you...."

Ice shook right, then rolled left, thinking he had DeAndre beaten. DeAndre reached out and tapped the ball free of Ice's dribble. Ice kept moving while DeAndre picked up the dribble and headed straight for the basket. He hopped and slammed down a two-handed dunk that shook the ground.

He took the ball out. When Ice faced him, DeAndre asked, "What do you think now?"

Ice snarled, still determined, "You ain't no Jordan."

DeAndre inbounded to Danny then clapped for the ball back. He back Ice down. "I might not be Jordan to the rest of the world, but I am to you."

DeAndre felt another body near him. Ice and another guy were double teaming him. He looked and saw Sidewinder wide open at the three-point-line. DeAndre hooked a pass to him. Sidewinder caught the ball and held it. Ice's team recovered quickly and ran over to pressure him. Sidewinder passed the ball to Chino who popped a shot and missed.

Choppy grabbed he rebound, and seconds later Ice's team was up two, one.

"C'mon, Sidewinder!" DeAndre shouted as he approached him. "You have to take those open shots. When they're double-teaming me, it means one of you guys is open. That's how we're going to win."

"I'm sorry. I-I..."

"Don't worry about it, "DeAndre continued. "We can't worry about the last point, only the next one. Just play your game, move the ball, and take your open shot. That's all you have to do."

Choppy took the ball out. Ice's team moved the ball well and inched closer to the goal. Ice backed Danny down and rolled around him for a lay-up, but he missed. Danny snatched the rebound and tossed it down court to Chino. Chino was well guarded by Ice, so he passed to DeAndre who shot an easy three-pointer.

They traded points for a few exchanges, but DeAndre's team passed him the ball with each possession. He always made the shot, but as the game went on, he felt that they were depending on him too much.

Ice took the ball out. "Seven, nine." He declared. He passed the ball to Choppy.

Danny was quick to engage Choppy. Instead of walking Danny down he kept him at a distance while dribbling. "You can't guard me, boy," he taunted. Choppy faked left then crossed over behind his back to the right. Danny tripped over his own feet, and Choppy ran in for the easy lay-up.

Choppy took the ball out this time. "Eight, nine." He inbounded to Ice. Ice moved the ball around. It came back to him. He shot at the top of the key, right in Sidewinder's face. Swish. "C'mon, y'all!" DeAndre prodded. "We let them tie this game up. We should have won already. Danny, tighten up on your D. Sidewinder, pay attention. Don't let him shoot your eyes out without a challenge."

Ice stood out of bounds ready to play. "Game point." He passed the ball to Choppy.

This time Danny was aggressive. He crowed Choppy so tightly that the man couldn't move. Instead of passing the ball, Choppy tried to dribble around him.

Danny reached out and slapped the ball away. It bounced right to Chino.

Chino took the ball and froze. No one guarded him, yet he stood stark still and staring as if he didn't know what to do.

"Shoot it!" DeAndre shouted.

When Chino finally got the ball, Choppy was there to block it. Ice scooped up the ball and shot it to score the game winning point.

Get off our court, chumps!" Choppy yelled.

Chino wouldn't meet anyone's eyes on the sidelines.

DeAndre approached him. "Why didn't you take the shot?"

"Because I couldn't make it."

"How did you know that?"

"I'm not like you, DeAndre. Everything I shoot won't go in."

DeAndre took a long look at him. Chino's eyes were red. His lower lip trembled.

Chino sat on a weight bench, so DeAndre sat beside him. "You're not going to make every shot, but that shouldn't stop you from trying. I won't always be open. You're our best shooter. You have to be our secret weapon. The other teams will focus on me. You'll be like a wolf in a chicken coop.

Chino finally looked at him. "You think I can be a secret weapon?"

DeAndre nodded. "Damn right."

Chino smiled. "I'll try to play better next time."

"That's all I can ask."

Preach called out to DeAndre from near the exit door. DeAndre put on his pants and walked over. "They've been calling you over the intercom for legal mail." Preach told him.

DeAndre tried to read the excitement in Preaches eyes. Then it dawned on him. "The judge ruled on my case."

"Maybe."

They started walking through the gym. "What else could it be?"

The trip to regular population was a long one. DeAndre wanted to be happy, but there was so much ambiguity. The judge's ruling could go either way. He hoped he would get a new trial, but there was not a way to be certain if it would happen. He'd have to open the letter and find out.

The legal mail lady was on the first floor waiting for him in the lobby outside of the Sargent's office. He signed his name in the logbook, and she handed him a white envelope. The return address read HAROLD JACKSON, Wake County Superior Court Justice.

He ripped the envelop open but hesitated to read it. He felt like Chino must have felt, holding the ball, afraid to find out if he could make the shot or not.

"What does it say?" Preach asked him.

DeAndre scanned the first page. One word stood out. DENIED. DeAndre saw it and the letter dropped to his side.

"What is it?" Preach asked.

Instead of replying, DeAndre handed him the letter. Preach didn't skim over the paper, he read every single word. After finishing, Preach lowered the letter with a sigh. "He denied you because he claims that your appellate attorney could have made the same argument during your direct appeal. It's typical. His way of not wanting to answer on the merits of your claim. He could have given you an evidentiary hearing, when he would have been forced to call your friend Michael as a witness. If he recanted his statement, you'd have a claim for actual innocence. By denying you on the technicality he avoided all of that."

"That's not right."

"No, it's not. But I told you before that you had a better chance of losing than winning. It's not over. We can appeal."

DeAndre hung his head low. He'd given everything he had. Hope was not an easy thing to have in prison while he was surrounded by so much hopelessness. "I don't know if I have the energy, Preach. It feels like I'm going to die in here."

Preach clasped a hand to his shoulder. "You face though teams, right? How did you beat them?"

"I don't know. I dug down deep and found a way to win. I never gave up."

"I need you to have that same energy right now. Keep fighting. Trust me. You don't want to be sitting here twenty years from now wandering what could have been. If you lose, you lose. Don't quit. If you quit...you've beaten yourself."

DeAndre was headed up the stairwell with the judgement in his hand as the Captain and Lieutenant were walking Officer Martin down in handcuffs. Each ranking officer had a firm hand locked around one of her elbows as if she would sprout wings and fly away from them. Her tear-reddened eyes were downcast in shame.

Breath ceased in DeAndre's lungs. "Martin! What's going on?"

When she looked up, a fresh valley of tears fell from her eyes. "I'm sorry, DeAndre," she said. "I messed up. They made me do it. I didn't think I had a choice."

Their progress came to a halt when they reached DeAndre. The Captain beefed up his chest. "Out of the way, son. Unless you want to go to the hole for interfering with an officer's duties." DeAndre didn't want to let them pass, yet if he didn't, he knew that it wouldn't make the situation any better. He stepped aside with a million questions plaguing his mind. He focused on one, but he couldn't ask it. Martin was already fired. That fact was obvious. Prying in front of her superiors could only get her in more trouble. He watched silently as they walked down and rounded another flight.

Before disappearing, Martin stared up at him. She mouthed no goodbyes, just looked at him. Then she was gone.

DeAndre stood on the stairs, remembering that last look. It was a look that contained a combination of hurt, love, regret, sadness and shame.

He sprinted up the stairs, determined to find out why Martin had been fired.

Officer Johnson was stationed on his housing floor. She sat at her desk, ramrod straight, eyes forward and in a daze. DeAndre flung the door open and stalked into the lobby.

He planted both hands on the desk. "Tell me what happened!"

Johnson's eyes were slick with new tears, her gaze lowered to the desk's wooden surface. "I don't know."

DeAndre slapped the desk. "Don't lie to me. She was your friend. You know how much I cared about her."

Johnson's glassy eyes rose to meet his. "All I know is that she got caught with some tobacco. Somebody snitched on her. They let her bring it into the building, then they ran up on her. The administration had to know beforehand. They had to."

Despite the revelation, DeAndre wasn't upset at the officers who had set Martin up. "Who was she bringing tobacco to?"

Questions turned in DeAndre's mind like cogs in a grandfather clock. He couldn't get the image of Martin sharing the bond they had shared with some random prisoners out of his mind. Wasn't she smarter than that? He knew that she would break the rules. She'd brought him legal materials. Would she do it for someone else? He couldn't help but question her loyalty to him. Then again, what reason did she have to be loyal to him? He wasn't her boyfriend. Still... there was nothing worse than thinking he couldn't trust someone that he cared for.

DeAndre stood up. "I can't believe she would do this to me."

"No," Johnson assured him. "She didn't do it because she wanted to. She did it because I needed help."

"You, help with what?"

Johnson pursed her lips. Her fingers fumbled in her lap.

DeAndre slapped the table again, this time hard enough to make her jump. "What was she helping you do, and why?"

"The prison had me under investigation. I'd been bringing in stuff for a long time, and I never got caught. Not one time. It's been going on for years. But I guess the wrong person got wind of it."

"Did anyone tell you were being investigated?"

"They singled me out one day when I reported to work. The searched my lunch bag, but everything else just walked on through. The other day they said they had to strip-search me."

DeAndre had to agree that the prison's actions were suspicious. "But what did that have to do with Martin?"

"I couldn't stop, DeAndre. I was getting paid regularly to bring stuff in here. Most of the time it was five-hundred dollars a month. It might not seem worth it to you, but I have four kids at home and no one to help me take care of them. Hustling here was like having a second job. My kids needed things that this place doesn't help me to afford. I had to do something."

DeAndre rubbed his eyes. "Johnson. You're not talking to the Warden or an investigator. I don't care how many kids you have or if they're eating you out of house and home. Why was Martin bringing tobacco in here?"

"I couldn't risk getting fired. I asked Martin to do it for me. I asked her to just get it in through the front gate. I would take it from her in the bathroom. She didn't want to do it. She said that she didn't want to jeopardize the relationship that she had with you. No matter what I said, she refused to help me."

DeAndre looked from Johnson, finding it hard to meet her eyes. "Something changed her mind."

Johnson winced at his words. "He...convinced her."

DeAndre froze in place, a man's face clear in his mind. "He?"

Fresh tears fell down Johnson's cheeks. "He tried to pressure her before, but it didn't work. She wouldn't do it, and he let it slide. Why, I don't know. But this time he was serious, and she knew it."

****

"Gator told her he was going to have me killed if she didn't mule for him." He paced laps around his small cell. Preach stood at the door, leaning against the front with his arms crossed.

Preach sighed. "He's done this type of thing before, hasn't he?"

DeAndre nodded. "Yeah. I told her not to get involved then, no matter what happened. I don't know why she did it. It does not make any sense."

"Sure, it does. She didn't care for you then as much as she does now."

"If that was true, she would have done all she could to keep us together. Instead, she..."

Preach threw up his arms. "Man, you didn't hear a word I just said, did you? If money is the root of all evil, love is the cause of all irrational thought. I killed a man because I loved my sister so much. Your mama kept knowledge of me hidden because she loved you. You refused to tell on your best friend, so now you're doing life for a crime he committed. Martin wasn't thinking about getting caught, or even that you might be separated if she did. She was thinking about keeping you alive. That's all."

DeAndre punched his fist into his palm. The ugly side of prison kept showing its snarling face. He was convinced that being incarcerated was not the sole nor the worst punishment of prison. No. The system had to take from him in every capacity. Opportunity. Life. Humanity. Love. He'd been stripped of every experience of decency, and by no fault of his own. Each day that passed presented another virtue to be stripped away. It made him careless and less about life.

He stopped pacing to look Preach in the eye. "I need a knife."

"Are we going through this again?"

DeAndre gritted his teeth. "If I had done it before, I wouldn't be in this situation now. I listened to you and Martin is fired because of it."

"Nah, DeAndre. Martin got fired because she wasn't strong enough to say no."

I don't understand why you're blaming her. Gator caused these problems. He orchestrated all of this to get at me."

Preach shook his head. "Listen to yourself. This has nothing to do with you. It's about one man's greed and his desire to get what he wants at all costs. Gator is a tornado moving from town to town with nothing but destruction on his mind. You're a pawn in his game, not a king. And don't get me wrong. I'm not blaming Martin. She had options she could have explored. She could have reported it. She could have quit. She chose to do what he wanted. That's why she lost her job. If you keep on this tirade, you'll self-destruct too."

"Something has to be done. I can't do anything."

Preach stepped off the door frame and into the cell. "Let's say you stab Gator. Matter of fact let's say you killed him. Then what?"

DeAndre almost smiled at the thought. "Then I would have what I want."

"Revenge?"

"If you want to call it that."

"Okay. Guess what? Martin will still be fired. You'll still be serving life in prison. On top of that, you'll be on Supermax for ten or twenty years. Probably get a fresh life sentence too. All of your chances to get out will be gone. Yeah, that's right. Keep that stupid look on your face. I've been around a lot longer than you. Gator didn't create himself. He' a product of the system. They toss smart young men in here with no opportunities and no hope, and they find a way to thrive the best way they know how. They come in here with no outside help and no release date, and the state expects them to do right because a clown in a uniform tells him to. There's a Gator in every prison. Most of the time there are several. If you're going to kill one, you might as well kill them all." Preach slid a sharpened steel rod from his pants and held it out to DeAndre. "Take it, if you want. But think about the drama that comes with it."

CHAPTER
SIXTEEN

A week without Martin seemed to be the longest of his life. He felt drained and spent every waking moment. Most days he didn't want to get out of bed, and if he did, it was only because he had to. Her absence left a void in his life that he didn't know how to fill.

There was a knock at his door. DeAndre looked up and saw Danny standing there. He got up and opened his cell door. As usual, Danny said nothing.

DeAndre sat on his bunk and rubbed sleep from his eyes. "I'm not playing in the tournament today. Tell everybody that I'm sorry. I don't have the energy."

Danny stood there. He let out a sigh and dropped his eyes.

"Did you hear me?" DeAndre asked him.

"I heard you, "Danny told him." But you, lying in bed all day isn't going to bring her back."

DeAndre's shock didn't come from the fact that he had heard Danny's voice for the first time, but that Denny was talking to him about Martin. "What makes you think that I'm not playing because of a woman?"

He eased into DeAndre's cell and sat on the toilet. "Everybody knows that you and Martin were cool. The walls whisper. There aren't too many secrets in prison."

"Okay. You know, so what?

"I didn't come here to argue with you."

"Why did you come?"

"To be your friend."

DeAndre chuckled. "Danny, you barely talk. What do you know about friendship?"

"I know how easy it is to feel you're the only person on earth to have ever fallen in love and lost it. Meeting a woman in prison is tragic because you can't do what you want, say what you sant, or be yourself. You always have to look over your shoulder. And just when you find a way to make it work, she's snatched away." Danny looked off, not space. "It's the worst feeling in the world."

"You talk like you've been there before."

Danny met his stare with sober eyes. "I have. She was my first and only love. I've been locked up since I was thirteen. I never hugged a girl when I was on the street."

DeAndre stared at him while trying to imagine an existence without love, only the isolation of prison. The only time DeAndre had touched someone in the time he'd been locked up was during the few skirmishes he'd been forced in to. Yet here was a man who knew no other way of life.

"What happened? Did she get fired trying to bring you something?"

"Nah." What would pass for a half-smile spread across Danny's lips. "I would have never asked her to do that. We got caught kissing. It turned out to be pretty bad." He trailed off and let the memory commandeer his words. The corners of his smile sank into a frown. "I didn't want to live after she quit. Every time I laid down for sleep, it felt like a pile of bricks was stacked on my chest. It took a long time for that type of pain and anxiety to go away, but it did, and life got easier."

"Yeah? How?"

Danny held up his left hand and jiggled his wedding band. "Her first letter came a few weeks later. After that, we wrote every day. I transferred to another prison, and she was able to visit me. She asked me to marry her a year later. Now she's working with my lawyer to get me out of here."

DeAndre swore that he saw a golden aura of happiness glowing all over Danny. The love of his life explained a lot about why he was who he was, without explaining anything at all. He didn't search for temporary friendships or money or drugs to help pass mundane days behind prison walls. He was not stuck in the miserable present of prison life. He was focused on a future of love and promise that only he could see. Such a revelation was inspiring but damning all the same.

"I told you that..." Danny continued. "Because you need to know that the good way, she made me feel doesn't have to end. If she cares about you, you'll hear from here. And it'll be better because you won't have to look over your shoulder every time, she makes you smile."

No matter how hard DeAndre hoped that would happen, he couldn't be sure. "What if I don't hear from her?"

Danny raised his eyebrows. "Then you have to keep living your life. You're not going to die because Martin moves on. If can't be easy loving a man serving life in prison. It's more likely that she'll find a man out there. I now you didn't want to hear that, but it's true, and you can't let it dictate your actions. I've seen guys kill themselves after a woman has left them. I mean, we don't have much to hold on to as it is. The one thing we thought was secure goes away, it's hard to handle. I guess the key is to let go if you have to. Holding onto something you can't have only makes it worse."

Danny didn't appear as ancient as his wisdom. He'd spoken like a man who knew what it was like to have a broken heart, to piece it all together again.

Danny stood. "I have to go." He reached into his pocket and handed DeAndre an envelope. "I told preach that I was coming up here to talk to you, and he asked me to give you this."

He stared at the envelope in his hand. "What is it?"

"I don't know. He said that you need to read it and then send it off."

DeAndre opened the envelop. Inside was a handwritten legal document entitled 'Writ of Certiorari, addressed to The North Carolina Court of Appeals." He read the first few lines and realized that it was the appeal he needed to file. He'd been so depressed that it had slipped his mind.

Danny walked to DeAndre's cell door. "I'll tell Chino and Sidewinder that you can't make it to the tournament."

"Wait, a second. Don't tell them that." He smiled. "Tell them that I'll be down there in a minute."

After Danny left, DeAndre read over the appeal Preach had written for him. It was short, well-written, and on point. He stared at the papers in his hand with fresh tears streaming down his face. He thought about all the birthdays, graduations, and events Preach had missed. Martin's absence had left a well of a hole in his life. Preaches absence had left an ocean. But with this one motion, it all seemed okay. Preach could not give him back the life he'd never had, but the old man was trying his best to give him back the best life that he could have. A life of freedom.

He dropped the appeal in the mailbox on his way to the yard.

***

The recreation yard was packed with prisoners and a peppering of staff. One gym worker handed out red and white bags of popcorn to spectators while another squirted juice from a yellow cooler into Styrofoam cups. A small stage was set up beside the court with a digital scoreboard and a folding table for men to take stats of the game. Off to the side of the stage, an inmate broadcasted announcements through a microphone and a small amplifier.

Gator's team, announced as 'The Pretty Tonys', was the first called to the court. His seven-man squad stepped out wearing fresh white sneakers. They had fresh haircuts, twisted dreds, and clean French braids. Every one of them was a gang member and Gator's flunky. Gator stepped out with them at first, then walked back to the coach chair on their bench.

They faced a formidable squad of six who had chosen to name themselves 'The Dominators'.

Two civilian referees called the game, a tall black female, and a short white male.

The game began slow, with each team trying to find a rhythm and feel out their opponent. The Pretty Tonys played conservative at first, though it was clear to DeAndre that the Dominators were the weaker team. Not only were they less skilled, they were intimidated. He noticed that the Dominators did all they could to avoid making contact with The Pretty Tonys, even though The Pretty Tonys were playing a style of basketball resembling a bloody rugby match.

The refs called few fouls and none against The Pretty Tonys. During one exchange, Keyvon pushed one of the Dominators down and yanked the ball out of his hands. No call. He then ran up the court cradling the ball like a newborn baby, not dribbling, and twisted into a 360-degree dunk. No traveling.

DeAndre and his team sat silently in the bleachers until the final buzzer rang and Gator stepped onto the court yelling. "Ain't no need to play no more games! Just give us the championship and ain't nobody gotta break a sweat! No harm, no foul!" The Pretty Tonys crowded around him chanting "We Ready!" as they celebrated.

Sidewinder turned to DeAndre wearing wide eyes. "That's what we're up against?"

DeAndre had no words of encouragement to console him. "I guess so."

The final score was seventy-eight to fifteen. Two Dominators limped off the court. A third clamped his nose closed to keep it from spewing blood all over the place.

That wasn't a game," Chino said. "It was a Zombie Apocalypse. Let one of them elbow me like that. It'll look like a UFC fight out there. I don't care what gang they represent."

The announcer called out, "DeAndre Harris! Approach the stage!"

"That's us," DeAndre said. His team fallowed him to the stage.

The inmate basketball commissioner cocked his head as he stared pitifully at DeAndre's team. "Sorry, man, but I'amma have to disqualify y'all."

DeAndre glanced at his boys, then back to the commissioner. "Why?"

"You only have four players. This is five on five."

"What does that mean?" Chino stepped in. "It's our disadvantage, not theirs. We should be able to run if we want to."

The commissioner shook his head. "Can't do it."

DeAndre scanned the bleachers and the spectators. He found it amazing that he wanted to play, now that chance may be taken away from him, yet two hours before he didn't want to get out of bed. "What if I can find another player?"

The commissioner glanced at his watch. "Your game starts in five minutes. One second late and you forfeit."

DeAndre hurried over to the bleachers where Preach and Percy were sitting. "Preach, I need you." He explained the situation.

"I can't help you," Preach said.

DeAndre looked to Percy.

Percy cocked one eyebrow. "Don't even fix your lips to ask me. I got arthritis, gangrene and hammer toe. Just watching y'all dribble that ball up and down the court got me aching."

"Preach," DeAndre tried again, "You don't even have to play. Run up and down the court. That's it."

Preach stared deeply into DeAndre's eyes. "There are some things you're going to have to do on your own. This is one of them."

A rumbling voice from the top of the bleachers bellowed. "I'll play with you." Bull stood up and pushed guys out of his way so he could step down."

DeAndre faced him, not knowing if he was serious or joking. "The last time we played you tried to knock my head off."

"That's because you were with Gator then. Now you're not."

"That makes all the difference, huh?"

Bull smiled. "Damn right."

They shook hands and headed toward the stage. The commissioner accepted Bull as their fifth player. "But what's your team name?"

Just then Gator and The Pretty Tonys strutted past. "Gator scowled at DeAndre. "Y'all scrubs ain't got a chance."

DeAndre followed them with his eyes. He told the commissioner, "Call us 'The Scrubs'."

The commissioner laughed. "The Scrubs? Wait… you're serious? All right. Next match up. The Scrubs versus 'The Hawks'."

Tip Off.

DeAndre stepped center court to face a Hawk for jump ball. The ref tossed it up. DeAndre tipped the ball to Chino who bolted toward their goal. A Hawk was hot on his heels and gaining on him. Chino when down for a lay-up, and the Hawk swatted the ball away. His teammate picked it up, and all ten players sprinted in the opposite direction.

The scrubs set up in a zone defense, where each player guarded a specific area instead of an individual player. Tough Bull had never played with them before. His instincts let him to a center position beneath the rim. The Hawks were forced to move the ball. One finally challenged Sidewinder and dribbled around him. Chino anticipated a lay-up and left his zone to pick the man up. Instead of charging Chino, he shuttled the ball to an open man in Chino's zone who drilled a three-pointer.

Chino took the ball out and passed it into DeAndre. "I should have stayed in my zone."

"Don't worry about it Chino." DeAndre told him as they moved up the court. "Slow it down. Don't let one player bother you. We've got a long game to play."

They set up at half court. DeAndre passed the ball to Sidewinder. A Hawk pressed him defensively, stole the ball, then dunked it before Sidewinder had a chance to dribble two times.

The crowd roared while pointing at the Scrubs and jeering.

The rest of the first half went much the same way. The two teams walked off the court with the score standing at thirty-five to fifteen.

"We're getting murdered," Sidewinder said after draining a cup of juice.

"I thought we were doing pretty good," DeAndre told him.

"That's easy for you to say," Chino butted in. "You scored all fifteen points. The rest of us suck."

Bull paced in front of the bench with his muscles rippling and drenched in sweat. "I ain't sign up to get whupped in the first round. I can go back and sit in the bleachers if ya'll ain't gonna try to win. Y'all got me out here looking like a straight sucker.

DeAndre knelt on the concrete before them. "Bull's right."

"They're picking apart our zone defense. "Chino said. "We need to go man-to-man."

"I don't know." DeAndre looked to Sidewinder.

"I can keep up," Sidewinder assured him. "I won't let you down."

DeAndre looked to Danny. "You with it?"

Danny nodded.

"Okay, but to play man-to-man you have to play them close. Chino stop being so anxious. I know they're pressing you, but slow down on the dribble. Look for an open man to pass to before you drive. Danny. You're the quickest on the team. Run our man around to see if you can draw a double team and leave one of us an open shot. Sidewinder, when you get the ball, shoot. I don't care if the Statue of Liberty is trying to block your shot. Take it and make it. "He looked to Bull." You just look mean and ugly."

The ref blew the whistle to signify the start of the second half. The Scrubs stepped onto the court, standing taller and with a renewed purpose."

Chino inbounded to DeAndre who dribbled to the top of the key. DeAndre gave them time to set up. He bounces-passed to Danny. Danny didn't hesitate to drive to the basket, weaving through Hawks for an easy lay-up.

The Hawks brought the ball back up the court. Each Scrub picked a man and played him close. Instead of chasing The Hawks around the court, they blocked their paths at every turn.

The Hawks couldn't gain an advantage. One was forced to lob a sloppy two-pointer from the top of the key. Danny rebounded and slung it to Chino. He hustled up the court, but instead of trying a rushed lay up, as he had before, he slowed down and let his team catch up. Two Hawks double-teamed DeAndre, leaving Sidewinder wide open near the sidelines. Chino flipped the ball to sidewinder who dropped a clean three as soon as the ball touched his hands.

"I made it!" Sidewinder shouted, running up the court beside Danny. "It was easier than I thought."

Danny laughed. "I know. Now do it again."

The next few weeks were a blur of basketball. DeAndre hadn't played so much since the NCAA Tournament. The main difference was that he wasn't playing on a blue-chip team destined for greatness. Every game was an uphill climb that left DeAndre and the Scrubs drained, but somehow victorious. Game after game raised the prison's level of respect for the clowns DeAndre had turned into contenders.

Gator's The Pretty Tonys owned the other half of the bracket, demolishing their opponents by striking fear into them. None offered a viable challenge to the throne.

At the end of one month's play, it was The Scrubs and The Pretty Tonys set to play the championship game.

DeAndre stepped onto the yard. His team was already on the sidelines stretching and warming up. Preach met him about center court, wearing a proud smile, and asked, "You ready?"

DeAndre mirrored his father's grin. "I'm always ready."

"You know that Gator is bringing a lot more than basketball to this tournament."

DeAndre's frown flatlined. "Are you telling me to throw the game?"

He clapped a hand on DeAndre's shoulder. "Are you kidding me? This is the first time I've really seen you play ball besides watching you on TV. I'm telling you to watch your back when you win. That's all."

They laughed. DeAndre gave Preach a hug, then walked to the sidelines. He was pulling off his uniform pants when Gator approached. "Schoolboy." He gestured to the Scrubs getting ready to play. "You took the bums that couldn't get in Sunday morning pickup games and brought them all the way to the top. You should be proud of yourself."

"What do you want, Gator? I need to meet with my team."

Gator stepped closer. "Listen, bro. I have a lot of money riding on this game. What do you have? Think about how upset I'll be if you luck up and win and cost me a grip?"

DeAndre raised an eyebrow. "Luck, huh?"

"But you can make sure it doesn't happen." Gator whispered. "If you do, I'll break you off a little something for your trouble."

DeAndre spoke loud enough for his team to hear him. "I've learned a lot in the short year that I've been pulling time, Gator. I know what I'm up against. You can't score or buy me out of this game. I'm my own man, and I came to win."

A grimace trembled across Gator's lips. "I want you to remember that you said that. You hear me? Remember, every single word.

DeAndre turned his back as Gator backed away.

Gator called out, "Hope y'all got some helmets and shoulder pads. I heard it could get violent out there."

"What was that all about?" Chino asked once DeAndre settled into a chair.

"It's not important."

"It is." Chino responded. "One of Gator's boys approached me this morning saying the same thing, trying to scare me."

DeAndre paused. "What did he say would happen if we won?"

"He didn't, but I knew what he was saying."

He gathered the team into a tight huddle. He asked, "Has anybody else been approached by Gator or his people?"

Everybody nodded except Bull. "He knows better than to try me."

"We have a choice to make." DeAndre looked each of them in the eye." Gator is going to pressure us. That's a given. I can't speak for the rest of ya'll, but I can handle it. If anybody doesn't want to play, we can forfeit right now."

Sidewinder shook his head. "I ain't quittin."

"Me neither" Chino said.

Danny just shrugged.

"All right. If we set foot on that court, there is no turning back. We have to win. This is the worst it's ever going to get. They're going to push us around. They're going to try to hurt us. Don't be intimidated. Play you game. They can's contest against points."

Sidewinder frowned. "What if they punch us?"

"Run up the score. Fighting can't win a basketball game. Baskets do."

Tip Off.

DeAndre met Keyvon in the center for jump-ball. Keyvon said nothing. He stared DeAndre down like a fighter in the middle of a boxing ring.

A female ref eased between them and tossed the ball into the air. When DeAndre jumped, Keyvon shoved him to the ground, caught the ball when it came down, then passed to Deadman who hustled down the court and dropped an easy dunk.

Keyvon stood over DeAndre snarling. "Stay there so I don't have to keep knocking you back down."

Danny ran over and pushed Keyvon out of the way. He helped DeAndre up. "You okay?"

DeAndre dusted himself off. "I will be."

They didn't have time to talk about it. Sidewinder inbounded to Chino. They trotted up the court, and Chino gave his team time to set up. DeAndre called for the ball by clapping. Chino passed it to him in a corner behind the three-point line. Keyvon was quick to engage him and swatted at the ball as DeAndre stooped in a dribble.

"Schoolboy." Keyvon taunted. "I've been waiting on this."

DeAndre looked him dead in the eye. "Hop it was worth the wait."

He jerked left, then right. Keyvon stayed with him, never giving an inch. DeAndre drove straight into him and Keyvon didn't back down. Finally, DeAndre pressed his back into Keyvon's chest and was able to swivel around him.

Deadman picked him up two steps toward the basket to box him in. DeAndre spotted Sidewinder wide open across the court and launched the ball at him. Swish. Their first bucket was an easy three-pointer.

Danny ran beside DeAndre as they hustled up the court. "You're going to have trouble with him, huh?"

"Nah." DeAndre panted. "I went up against better defense in Junior high school. I was just feeling him out. I'm about to show y'all something you've never seen before."

Danny was smiling like a jack-o-lantern. "What's that?"

"Watch and you'll see."

Keyvon brought the ball up the court. DeAndre picked him up at half court. Keyvon dribbled behind his legs to keep the ball away. "Oh, you think you can guard me, Schoolboy? I'mma show you how we..."

DeAndre reached out, slapped the ball away from Keyvon and scooped it up on his way to a wide-open goal. He hopped from the free-throw line, threaded the ball through his legs, and dunked hard enough to make the ground shake.

The crowd erupted.

Gator paced up and down the sidelines with his hands on his hips. DeAndre trotted past him and shouted, "This is my court!" Gator only stared.

Three minutes later The Scrubs were up eighteen to six when Gator called a timeout.

The Scrubs were chattering excitedly on the sidelines.

"We're tearing them up!" Chino declared.

"I can't believe this is real!" Sidewinder added.

"Don't get too happy." DeAndre told them. He glanced down the court and saw Gator talking to his team. He couldn't hear what was being said, but the way Gator was flapping his arms made it look like a serious situation. "They're down there planning something."

Chino chuckled. "They're strapping on brass knuckles."

Sidewinder laughed along with him.

 DeAndre kept a straight face. "It's funny, but he's right. I told y'all that they couldn't beat us straight up. Now they're going to bully us."

"I'm the only bully on the court." Bull said.

"I'll agree with that but be on point. It's about to get rough."

The Pretty Tonys took out the ball after the timeout. Danny picked up Deadman as he dribbled down the court. Danny had the best defense on the team. When Deadman couldn't shake him, he put his back into Danny's chest, then spun and slammed his elbow hard into Danny's eye. Danny went down and Deadman leapt over him to put up an easy lay-up.

Chino ran up on the ref. "Didn't you see that?"

The ref ignored him and ran up the court.

DeAndre helped Danny to his feet. The white of Danny's left eye was bright red. "You alright?"

Danny tried to blink away the pain. "Never better. Let's play ball."

The ref blew the whistle. Sidewinder passed the ball to Bull who ran straight up the court and into the converging bodies of three Pretty Tonys as he leapt for a layup and missed.

Keyvon snatched the rebound and headed the other way. DeAndre blocked his path beneath the Tonys' goal. Instead of trying to maneuver around DeAndre, Keyvon dipped his shoulder and rammed into DeAndre's chest, sending him flying backward and onto his back. Keyvon made an easy jump shot once DeAndre was out of the way.

Sidewinder screamed at the ref. "What about a charge, bro? He can't do that."

The ref backpedaled past him. "Y'all are grown men. Play ball. If you keep complaining, I'll through you out of the game."

"What?" Sidewinder shouted. Chino had to grab him to keep him quiet.

Gator heard the exchange and applauded as hard as he could. "That's right, ref! Tell him again! Play ball suckers! If you can't handle it, quit!"

The remainder of the first half went much the same way. By the sound of the half-time buzzer the score was close. Twenty-nine to twenty-three, The Pretty Tonys' way.

Bull was the only scrub who wasn't bleeding or wincing from pain during half time. He'd taken some abuse too but walked away unscathed.

Preach and Percy walked over.

Percy told Chino, "You need to stop letting that boy beat up on you like that."

Chino glared at him. "What would you do differently? Since you know so much."

"Stop lettin him use your head as a speed bag you bubble-lipped boy. The next time he punches you, punch him back. If he pushes you down, push him back. That's the only way you'll earn their respect."

"I don't want their respect." Sidewinder said. "I want to win."

Preach nodded. "you're going to have to stand up and be a man."

The buzzer sounded to signal the end of halftime. Preach and Percy went back to their seats.

DeAndre told his team, "I never lost a game, that I didn't leave drained and dog-tired. I don't plan to change that now. If they want a fight, then we'll give them a fight."

Everyone agreed.

Chino inbounded the ball to Danny. Danny got it to Sidewinder, who drilled a three-pointer as soon as he caught the ball. Deadman watched the ball go through the hoop and slammed his shoulder into Sidewinder's chest. Instead of cowering, Sidewinder slammed his shoulder into Deadman's chest.

"What's wrong with you?" Deadman asked him.

Sidewinder shrugged. "Same thing that's wrong with you." He ran up the court.

The Pretty Tonys had the ball. Keyvon got the rock. DeAndre pressed him by crowing in so close that Keyvon could barely dribble. Keyvon jammed his elbow into DeAndre's neck. DeAndre ignored the blow, yanked the ball out of Keyvon's hands, and passed it to Bull, who sprinted down the court for a smooth tomahawk dunk.

Keyvon shoved DeAndre then threw up his hands, ready to throw blows. DeAndre did the same. The ref blew her whistle.

Gator yelled out to Keyvon, "Play ball, bro! Don't let them take you out of your game!"

Reluctantly, Keyvon lowered his hands. "Wait till the game is over."

"I'll be ready."

They played the second half with a mutual understanding. If the Pretty Tonys wanted to play rough, then The Scrubs would play the same. DeAndre and his team never stopped scoring. Their rapid ascent forced The Pretty Tonys to hunker down and play ball. If they didn't, the score would get out of control.

The Scrubs were only up by two with twenty seconds left on the clock. The Pretty Tonys had possession.

Keyvon passed the ball to Deadman. They hurried up the court and shuffled the ball around while repositioning for a better shot. Finally, Deadman shook loose of Sidewinder and nailed an arching three-pointer to put them up one point with seven seconds left on the clock.

DeAndre called the last time out. "They're banking on me taking the last shot," he told his team once they were huddled up. "So, make sure I get the ball, and I'll pass it to Sidewinder."

Sidewinder's eyes blinked as bright as headlights. "Why me?"

DeAndre laid a hand on his shoulder. "Because you can make it."

The buzzer sounded. Chino passed the ball to Bull. The Pretty Tonys were all over DeAndre, trying to make sure he didn't get the ball. Bull lobbed a high pass that only DeAndre's long arms could reach. Three Pretty Tonys crowded him, leaving Sidewinder open at the three-point line with less than two seconds on the clock.

DeAndre slung the ball to him. Sidewinder popped off an arching shot a millisecond before the buzzer rant. The ball hit the front rim, bounced straight up, hit the rim again, then rolled in for the game-winning three points.

The prison rushed the court. A crowd of men surrounded Sidewinder to congratulate him again, then rolled in for the game-winning three points.

The prisoners rushed the court. A crowd of men surrounded Sidewinder to congratulate him. Even a line of staff leaned against the wall, clapping and smiling at the impossibility of it all.

DeAndre spotted Preach moving toward him with a smile plastered to his face. He smiled too. But then... Preaches smile faded away as his eyes widened in horror. Instead of weaving through the crowd, Preach started shoving people out of the way to get to his son.

DeAndre followed Preaches gaze just in time to see the gleam of a shank in Keyvon's hand as he tried to stab him in the belly. It happened so fast that DeAndre didn't have time to react. But Preach was there? He grabbed Keyvon's wrist and punched him in the face at the same time... The shank clattered to the concrete ground, too far from DeAndre's reach.

Keyvon broke free and squared up with Preach in the center of the ball court. So much commotion had everyone's attention, but soon realized something sinister was going on and parted to give them room to fight.

"This won't be like last time, old man. "Keyvon taunted, oscillating in a circle.

Preach kept his eyes on Keyvon's shoulders, watching for the slightest movement, but didn't say a word.

Keyvon shot a quick jab. Preach slipped it to the outside and inched with short rabbit punches to Keyvon's ribs. When Keyvon dropped his hands to protect his body. Preach rocked him with a right hook that twisted Keyvon's face and laid him out on the ground.

Preach looked down on him. "You're right. It wasn't like the last time. You went down faster."

Gator ran over and picked up the shank. He pointed it at Preach. "I'm tired of you always in my business."

Preach squared up. "I'm not going to let you hurt my son. I'll die first."

"You're about to." Gator lunged.

Preach moved a moment to slow. The steel rod was buried three inches inside Preaches gut.

"Preach!" DeAndre cried out. He swung and hit Gator in the jaw.

Gator turned to face him but was still stunned. DeAndre pumped his fists into "Gator's face until the gangster's nose exploded and he balled up on the ground.

Deadman and the rest of Gator's crew ran over to help him, but Leach and a team of Correctional Officers were already there, wielding batons and pepper spray.

DeAndre submitted to the handcuffs. His last glimpse of Preach was of him writhing on the basketball court, clutching his belly as DeAndre was led toward the hole.

CHAPTER
EIGHTEEN

There was no real way to tell time when in the hole. They'd taken all of his property when they locked him up, including his nine-dollar Casio wristwatch. DeAndre counted the days by the rising and setting of the sun, but after a week or so, he lost track of the actual date.

He estimated the time of day by the intervals in which they brought his meals and mail. The squeaky food art usually rolled into the segregation unit for the first time before sunup, around five-thirty in the morning. Lunch came when the sun was high and beaming in DeAndre's window that was around noon. Dinner was served while the sun was still up, but late, spreading a long sliver of sunlight across his concrete cell floor. Mail was delivered on second shift, long after the sun had gone down, around eight or nine at night.

Until he went to the hole, he had no idea that time was so important to him. Many nights passed with him lying on his rack thinking about the occurrence of time and its relevancy to the human race. He reasoned that time was an invention of mankind. It may have been important to ancient farmers who needed to keep track of seasons, or hunters who were chronicling the habits of animals, but the average prehistoric man had no use for time.

As a free man he'd been a slave to it. He always had somewhere to be, a class. practice, a game, a date. There was rarely a day when he didn't have a place to rush off to at a given moment or moment when he wasn't aware of what time it was. Time was his greatest motivator.

In prison, serving a life sentence, his time was useless. Convicts that had a release date had something to look forward to. If they chose, they could spend their days planning ahead toward an eventual date of release. For them, time was hope, and hope was the vitality of life. That's what they were waiting for; the day when they would get out and start a new life.

Not DeAndre. As the days ticked by it became easier and easier to throw away any hopeful thoughts.

When he tried to sleep, the minutes before he drifted off were filled with hazy visions of Keyvon and Deadman stomping him out in Gator's cell. He felt their boots making knobby imprints in his cheeks as he tried to ball up for protection. He saw Gator creeping on Preach with the shank in his hand, then the knife sinking into Preaches belly just as he turned to face his attacker. He saw thick black blood spurt out in gooey clumps. He tried to push the images out of his head. They would not leave. They only grew worse. His stomach tightened in painful convulsions that made him jackknife in bed, doubled over with his fingers clutching his abdomen. There were days when his meal trays sat on his desk, untouched and full until the guards came back to retrieve them.

If he was lucky enough to drift off into a slumber, he had an hour or so of peace until visions of Tabitha revealed themselves in the blackness of his sleep. He saw her in Chemistry I class, where they'd met. She sat two rows in front of him and wouldn't stop turning to smile his way. They took long walks at Pullen Park, went to the dollar theater off of Western Boulevard, and ate hotdogs in his car outside of Snoopy's restaurant. He dreamed all of these instances is if he were reliving every conversation, chuckle, or embrace that they shared.

A part of him knew they were only dreams, and he wished to stay in that coma-like state, never to return to the free world of the living. He would rather have been confined as a peaceful prisoner in his body than walk as a dead man in a United States prison.

Yet he always woke, clutching remnants of his dreams that sifted through his grasping fingers like wispy trails of smoke.

Sadness set in then. Inescapable sadness.

The course of his life made no sense. At this moment...he was supposed to be traveling the globe and considered the best athlete on the face of the earth, not wasting away in a concrete box.

It was on a horrid night when life was a black cloud in his sky that the letter came. He hadn't been expecting any mail. An officer arrived and slid a thick envelope in the thin space beneath his door, then walked away.

The name above the return address announced Michelle Maxton as the sender. DeAndre frowned when he read the name. He didn't know a Michelle Maxton, but as he opened the envelop, he realized who had written him.

Dear DeAndre,

Forgive me for not writing sooner, but I had to be sure that it was the right thing to do. I made a mess of things. There's nothing I can do to change it, and I'm sorry. I spoke to a friend, and she told me that she explained everything that I can't. Please understand that I only meant to protect you. I would have never compromised what we had intentionally.

This may come as a shock, but you are the only man I have ever loved. I have met many, but not one has affected me in the way that you have, and I intend to love you as long as you will let me.

He paused to smile at the white concrete wall. A million thoughts shuttled in and out of his head. The possibility that someone could live him during his darkest hour was mind-boggling, yet it was happening.

He thumbed through the pages. They were numbered all the way to sixteen. DeAndre laid down and settled his head into his pillow to finish reading. That night he slept the most peaceful, dreamless sleep that he'd known in his lifetime.

***

The visit came two days later.

If Martin's letter was a surprise, the two officers showing up at his door telling him that he had a visit was a shock. The Disciplinary Hearing Officer that convicted him of fighting had sentenced him to thirty days in the hole, ninety days with no phone and visiting privileges, eight hours extra duty, and had taken ten dollars out of his account for a fine. DeAndre didn't think he would get a visit for a long time.

Instead of Melody Martin or his mother waiting in the visiting booth, DeAndre sat across from a forty-ish white guy wearing a tailored suit. His black hair was combed and impeccable. He stared at DeAndre through sky-blue eyes that seemed to smile, through his lips did not.

"Who are you?" DeAndre asked as soon as the officers left him.

"How are you, Mr. Harris? My name is Richard Steinberg. I work for the office of Indigent Defense Services."

"I didn't uh I don't have the money to hire a lawyer."

Richard chuckled. "The IDS is a state entity, Mr. Harris. I've been appointed by the North Carolina Court of Appeals to contest your conviction in an evidentiary hearing."

DeAndre's heart was running a race in his chest. "I won my case?"

"Didn't you get a letter for the Court of Appeals?" DeAndre shook his head. "I'll make sure you get formal notification. But no, you haven't won your case... yet. The Writ of Certiorari that you filed was accepted in part by the Court. They have ordered the Wake County Superior Court to conduct an evidentiary hearing so they can garner more facts to better decide your case."

DeAndre's shoulders slumped. "It's still an uphill battle."

Richard offered a slight grin "It's always an uphill battle when you're young, black, and a polarizing figure such as yourself."

DeAndre thought about the lawyer's last statement. He was more than a Calvary come to assist him in the eleventh hour, he was a realist who saw the system exactly as it was. DeAndre couldn't have asked for a better attorney.

Richard went on. "Think about this though; an appellee has less than a ten-percent chance of winning a state appeal with a Writ of Certiorari. Especially one filed pro se by an inmate in prison, handwritten at that."

"I was lucky then, huh?"

"No. You don't get lucky in a court of law. Give yourself credit. You wrote a superb legal argument. It was well-researched and concise, exactly what a judge wants to read. Lawyers who have been practicing for decades never produce work that effective."

An image of Preach hunched over his little desk in his cell, shoving his reading glasses up over his nose, came to mind. He'd written the appeal in DeAndre's selfish absence, without help.

"I didn't write it," he admitted. "Someone else did."

"Another inmate?" DeAndre nodded. Richard shrugged. "I'd say you owe him an immense debt of gratitude. He has given me enough to run with. He may have given you a ticket out of here."

DeAndre couldn't help but smile. "It's that good?"

It all hinders on Michael Artiste." Richard flipped open a manila folder and skimmed a few lines. "The court wouldn't award you a new trial because there was no affidavit from him. Usually, that would be a necessity, seeing how your argument was based on disproving his claim that you killed your girlfriend."

"We went through my trial transcripts and printed out inconsistencies in his testimony. That was the best we could do," DeAndre said.

The lawyer nodded. "It was enough to get the court's attention. That's all that counts. I'll pick up the baton and contact Mr. Artiste see if I can get a statement from him."

DeAndre pinched the bridge of his nose and felt a headache coming on. "What if he won't admit that he lied on the stand?"

"It doesn't matter as much as you think. The object is to get any statement that compels him to testify at the evidentiary hearing. He'll have to recant his first testimony verbatim, without getting caught in a lie."

"Can you catch him in a lie?"

"I don't know. We'll take it one question at a time."

DeAndre liked what he was hearing. "What do you need me to do?"

"Right now? Nothing. Stay out of trouble. Stop going to the hole. I'll be in touch."

Richard Steinberg stood up to leave.

"Thank you," DeAndre told him.

"Don't thank me. I'm the last leg in this relay race. Thank the prisoner that wrote your appeal. He's the person who got you here. Not me."

***

DeAndre was released from the hole on the thirty-first day.

He was taken back to WRB and informed that he would be housed on the third floor in G-Block. That was the block Gator used to run. Instinct told DeAndre to protest, but he was in prison, and he couldn't run from a fight, so he carried his property bags up to stairwell, then enter G-Block.

Percy's was the first face he saw. The old man was sitting at a table with a chess board on top. His opponent's chair was unoccupied. He stared at the board with such concentration that he didn't notice DeAndre enter the cell block.

DeAndre sneaked up behind him. "I got next!"

Percy spun around and hopped up. "Hey, man!" He held out his hand for a shake. "We need to get you to a barbershop. You came out here looking like Wolfman Jack. Just might scare the kids."

DeAndre embraced him then pulled back. "There are kids here."

Percy lowered his voice to a whisper. "Don't tell the po-lice, then they wouldn't know how to treat us."

DeAndre laughed, then looked around the block. "How is Preach?"

Perry's smile faded. "Moving slow, but alive. He went to the bathroom. Be back in a minute. He'll be happy to see you."

"What about Gator?"

Don't worry about him. They locked up his whole crew. Sent them to different prisons all over the state. I think Gator is still here in the hole somewhere, but he'll be lucky to get out in the next year or so. Stabbing someone is serious business."

DeAndre didn't offer a reply. He stared at the floor in thought.

Percy laid a hand on his shoulder. "Youngblood don't worry about it. I know that you're looking years down the road when you'll run into them again. I wouldn't lose one wink of sleep. You can't predict the future."

DeAndre began to say thank you when he looked up and saw Preach walking toward him. Preach smiled as they embraced. "Am I glad to see you, Pop," DeAndre said. "I owe you a thanks you saved my life in many more ways than one."

CHAPTER
NINETEEN

DeAndre was led into the courtroom by two Sheriff's Deputies. He felt like an alien landing on earth for the first time when he stepped out of the back hallway wearing a Wake County orange jumpsuit. He hadn't seen normal people in so long. The professionals wore bland business suits. Spectators wore bright colors and shimmering jewelry. It was all overwhelming and foreign to him.

The next thing he noticed was the cleanliness of the courtroom. The wood-grained walls and desks were polished to a high sheen. The carpeting was clean and soft. Sunlight poured in through two open windows on both sides of the empty judge's bench. The place smelled like bleach and pledge, fresh and lemony.

His mother waved from the back bench. He looked over and saw her and Melody sitting nervously. On the other side of the courtroom were four cameramen filming him as he took his seat beside his lawyer. Assistant District Attorney Sandy Gillies sat sifting through papers at the table next to theirs. He was the same ADA that had tried DeAndre's murder trial. The look he gave DeAndre could have started a brush fire.

Richard Steinberg tapped him to draw his attention, then whispered, "I'm sorry that I didn't visit you when you came in this morning. I had to attend another evidentiary hearing."

"Did you win?"

"No. He went back to prison." Richard smiled at DeAndre's frown. "Don't worry about that. His case wasn't nearly as strong as yours."

"Glad to hear it. Do you think I could go home today?"

"That's not how it works. If the judge rules in your favor, he'll award you a new trial. You'll be housed in the County jail until the DA's office decides if they are going to retry. That's the reality of it; however, the chances of a re-trial are slim to none. With the new developments, there is no way they'd get a conviction."

"New developments."

"Michael Artiste is going to testify."

A storm of butterflies bounced off the wall of DeAndre's stomach. "You got the affidavit? What is he going to say?"

Richard leaned in closer to DeAndre's ear. "Well, a lot has transpired in his life during the past year."

"I know. He signed a rookie contract to the Milwaukee Bucks'. Probably bought a big house and a Bentley."

"Of course, that, but... he had some pretty interesting things to say."

"Things like what?"

"He claims that he actually..."

The Bailiff bellowed. "All rise!" Cutting Richard short.

The court stood as Judge Regal Walters strutted into the courtroom. He was a small man. Pale and slim with silver hair trimmed on the sides. Sky-blue eyes hid behind wire-rimmed spectacles. The man was no taller than five 'two', yet his towering stature captivated every soul in attendance. DeAndre knew Judge Walters well. He had been the justice that presided over his murder trial and sentenced him to life. They had a history indeed.

Judge Walters sat behind his bench. "You may be seated."

DeAndre was dying to hear what Richard had to say about Michael, but court was now in session, and he wouldn't dare disrupt it.

The judge looked to DeAndre's table. "Counselor Steinberg. Your client filed a paper writing a Motion for Appropriate Relief, in this court, alleging that a key witness made false testimony. That motion was denied. Your client then appealed to the North Carolina Court of Appeals, who granted Certiorari and ordered that this court hold an evidentiary hearing to bring the facts of the case to light. Do you wish to be heard further on the matter?"

Richard Steinberg stood tall with his back straight. "I do, your honor. I intend to prove that Michael Artiste, the State's only damning witness against my client, lied on the stand about his involvement in the killing of Tabitha Murray, resulting in the wrongful conviction of DeAndre Harris."

Sandy Gillies was on his feet. "Objection, your honor. For the record, Michael Artiste has never been proven as a false witness."

"That is true, your honor," Richard continued calmly." "But I filed a sworn affidavit from Michael Artiste admitting that he was the person who brought the murder weapon to the party that night, not DeAndre Harris. That is a complete contradiction of his earlier testimony."

"Your Honor," Gillis cut in. "There is no need to entertain this foolishness any further. Mr. Harris has been convicted. He lost his direct appeal there months ago. This evidentiary hearing is pointless. Mr. Harris has nothing to gain."

"Objection overruled," Judge Walters declared. "I understand your concern, Mr. Gillis, but we are here because the North Carolina Court of Appeals ordered it. For that reason, we will hear what Mr. Artiste has to say, and I will make my ruling based his testimony." He looked back to Richard. "Counselor Steinberg."

Richard's smile beamed bright enough to replace a lighthouse. "No need to prolong things any further. You honor, I would like to call Michael Artiste to the stand."

The Bailiff walked to a side door of the courtroom and opened it. Michael stepped out wearing a charcoal gray suite with a burgundy tie. His hair cut was fresh and the edges razor sharp. Two large diamonds dangled from his earlobes.

DeAndre noticed that he'd picked up muscle. A year in the NBA had transformed the scrawny twenty-something kid that DeAndre had once admired into a wealthy, gargantuan stranger.

There DeAndre sat, unkempt and malnourished from prison food. He was slim and weak. His hair was nappy and unruly, and he had a beard three days old and rugged. He wondered what he looked like to Michael. If he appeared to be even a shadow of what he once was? Regardless, Michael walked to the stand without looking DeAndre's way one time.

On the other hand, DeAndre's eyes never left Michael. He dared the man to look at him to see what he caused. It didn't matter that he was in prison and Michael was not. He would not allow himself one iota of jealousy. No amount of money could make Michael the man that DeAndre had become in the last year he'd spent in prison.

Richard didn't waste any time. "State your full name for the court."

"Michael Renaldo Artiste."

"And your occupation?"

"Do we really need to go through all this?" Michael asked the judge. "Everyone knows who I am."

Judge Willis leaned over to him. "It is a necessary formality, Mr. Artiste. You will answer every question posed to you truthfully, or I will hold you in contempt of court."

Michael rolled his eyes back to Richard. "I'm a professional basketball player. Right now, I am the starting shooting guard for the Milwaukee Bucks'"

"And remind the court about how you know DeAndre Harris."

Michael glanced at DeAndre for the first time, then quickly looked away. "We played ball together at NC State."

"Were you two friends?"

A hesitation, then a demure. "Best friends. We hung out every day since we were freshmen."

"Have you been in contact with Mr. Harris since his incarceration?"

Another hesitation. This one longer. "No."

"Is it safe to say that you two are not 'best' friends anymore?"

Sandy Gillies was on his feet. "Your honor, this line of questioning is irrelevant to the situation at hand."

Richard kept his eyes on Michael. "The nature of their relationship must be established."

"Your Honor," Sandy Gillies whined.

Judge Walters leaned over his desk toward the ADA. "Are you objecting, Mr. Gillis?"

"I am, your honor."

"Your objection is overruled. Counselor Steinberg, you may continue."

"Mr. Artiste," Richard went on. "Are you and DeAndre still friends?"

"No."

"Will you explain what ended your friendship?"

Michael grit his teeth as he peered around the courtroom. "I thought we were here to talk about what happened to Tabitha."

"We are, "Richard responded. "But please answer the question."

Michael's gaze locked on DeAndre's and stayed there. "We're not friends because of what happened to Tabitha. She got shot, and I testified against DeAndre."

"Ah. You testified that DeAndre Harris was the person that shot Tabitha Murray. Out of fifteen witnesses, you were the only one that claimed he saw DeAndre Harris with a firearm. You said that you saw him pull the trigger while aiming at a man he'd been engaged in a fight with, missing, and shooting his girlfriend in the head instead. Is that correct?"

Michael dropped his gaze. "It's true."

"But," Richard continued. "You state something completely different in your recent affidavit. Before we get into that, would you explain to the court what happened in your life to cause you to tell a different tale now?"

"I found Jesus."

"A little louder."

"I said that I found Jesus. My whole life was spent trying to be the best ballplayer that I could be. That's all I cared about. Nothing or no one else mattered. I had this dream that I would make it to the NBA and get super rich. The only thing that had ever threatened that dream was when Tabitha got killed.

"I testified against DeAndre, and that put me in the clear. I got drafted and earned a nice contract. Millions. I could never explain how good it felt to have so much money deposited into my bank account within the blink of an eye. I bought everything that I ever wanted. I got a mansion, cars, and I filled them with the best that money could buy I had women. I had everything, but I wasn't happy. The good feeling all those things brought me faded away with the newness of what I'd bought.

"And then my sister died. I had to go back to my old neighborhood to bury her, I saw so many familiar faces. People I used to love and who loved me. They looked at me in awe because I'd made it. I was rich, and no longer lived in the ghetto. They couldn't see my unhappiness.

"My childhood Pastor pulled me to the side to pray. I started crying, and we went to his office. We talked for a long time. He was the first person that I told."

Michael carried a single sheet of paper to Michael. "Do you recognize this?"

Michael nodded. "It's the affidavit I wrote in your office."

"You state in this affidavit that the only pistol you saw the night Tabitha was shot was your own. A complete contradiction of your testimony."

"That's right."

The crowd let out a collective gasp.

Richard went on. "Did DeAndre Harris have a firearm at all that night?"

Tears spilled from Michael's eyes as he stared at DeAndre. "No, sir. He asked me not to bring it in with us, but I did it anyway. He doesn't like guns."

Richard was like a pit bull on a flank steak. "And your firearm was the one that killed Tabitha Murry?"

"Some guys started trouble with DeAndre. Next thing you know, they were fighting. I meant to fire a warning shot, but somehow I fired into the crowd."

Gentle murmurings echoed throughout the courtroom. Judge Walters banged his gavel. "Order in the court."

Richard stepped in front of Michael full on. "Mr. Artiste. Please tell the court who fired the shot that killed Tabitha Murray."

Michael was sobbing now, finding it hard to catch his breath. "DeAndre didn't kill her. He's spent a year doing time when it should have been me. I robbed him of his shot. I's so sorry, DeAndre."

"Mr. Artiste. Who fired the shot that killed Tabitha Murray?"

"I did," Michael admitted. "I killed her."

CHAPTER
TWENTY

DeAndre entered the visitation booth, hoping that this time would be his last. He sat in the plastic chair and stared through the tiny window, waiting, as he had countless times before. It didn't take long for his thoughts to wander.

At that moment, he couldn't say that serving the last year of his life in prison had been such a bad thing. Sure, the conditions were antiquated, the food was horrible, and the days had been long, but the best thing that could have ever happened to him happened in prison.

He'd met his father.

Somehow that seemed worth the fact that he had almost been murdered in the process.

The wooden door on the other side of the visitation booth creaked open. Preach walked in wearing a crisp gray t-shirt, creased prison brown pants, and a toothy smile.

Leach filled the doorway behind him. He was grinning too. "What's up, boy? How's life on the other side of the fence?" His officer's badge gleamed in the sunlight.

"Harder than I remembered. I never thought about how little I had to worry about while I was in prison. No bills. No taxes. I mean, being locked up had its stresses, but in a different way."

Leach pondered that remark. He reached to his utility belt and whipped out his handcuffs. "You Wanna come back in?"

"Hell no! I fought for the responsibility that I have now, and I wouldn't trade it for the world."

Leach put his handcuffs away. "You never belonged here in the first place." He gave a nod to Preach, who had sat on his stool. "Have a good visit. I'll holler at you later." He closed the door, leaving them alone.

Preach turned to DeAndre with tears in his eyes. "Man, am I glad to see you out there instead of in here."

It had been seven months since he had left Central Prison to go to the evidentiary hearing. Three weeks later, the Wake County District Attorney's Office decided to dismiss the charges against DeAndre. He walked out of the County jail a free man.

Michael wasn't so lucky. As DeAndre was walking out, Michael was being led in, handcuffs behind his back, designer suit jacket draped over his head to shield his face from the camera crews and reporters trying to capture his image on their cell phones. They never crossed paths. DeAndre went out the front, Michael came in through the back. At his mom's house that night, he watched the story on the nightly news. Michael had been charged with first-degree murder.

Despite all he had been through, DeAndre still hated to see his friend behind bars. He'd been where Michael was headed, and he didn't wish that hell on anyone, not even his worst enemy. Regardless, it wasn't his problem anymore.

The North Carolina Department of Corrections wouldn't allow DeAndre to visit Preach until he had been removed from the correctional institution for six months. It was a blessing to be able to sit down with him, even if they had to be separated by a cinderblock wall.

So much had happened since he'd gotten out. DeAndre didn't know where to begin. He settled on, "You look good, Pop."

Preach grinned like he couldn't help it. "I feel good. Only the Lord knows how hard I prayed for this day. I've been in prison well over two decades, and I've been praying for half of that. I'm still here. But if you being a free man is the only prayer God answers, I will go to my grave the happiest man that ever lived, I'm telling you what!"

Salt water warmed DeAndre's eyes. "And I'm glad to be here to thank you for all that you did. I wouldn't be out here if it wasn't for you."

"It was only paper and ink, DeAndre. God whispered the words in my ear. All I did was write them down. He did the rest. My hand was the vessel for his will. I did nothing that he didn't want."

DeAndre wiped his eyes. "I'm not just talking about the law work. You kept me safe in here. Without you, there is no telling what Gator would have done to me. That and well, I never had a father. I grew up thinking I was fine without one, but when I spent time with you, I saw a side of myself that I never knew existed."

He remembered the night of his very first basketball game. He was six years old. His mother was working late and couldn't make it. "I'll be there as soon as I can be, "she'd told him. He rode to the game in the bed of his teammate's father's truck. He and his friend talked about their stats after the game, predicting how much they'd score and how everyone would live with them. DeAndre scored twenty-five points during the first half, and another thirty-seven in the second, setting a junior league record, and no one he cared about was there to see it. After the game he'd sat on the curb waiting for his mom to show up. He watched fathers pat their sons on the back while embracing them or explaining how they make their game better the next time. After all the fathers and sons had climbed in their cars and left for home, DeAndre hid his eyes and cried.

What drive and inspiration he couldn't get from a patriarch, he found in the form of coaches who treated him like a son. He worked harder than any other boy on his team, not trying to be the best, but to earn the praise of a father figure. Their attention was the only attention he wanted. When his mother couldn't make it to games, they took him out for pizza and ice cream after he'd demolished the rival team. He sat on booth bench seats alone, across from a father and son, dying inside because the vacant seat next to him would never be filled.

He grew up feeling fraudulent, despising his friends for the complaints they made about their fathers when he didn't have one. He felt like a thief, casing the relationships other boys had with their fathers like banks he planned to rob. Yet no matter what he did, he did not feel loved.

To supplement the void in his life, he filled it with basketball. He spent hours alone on empty courts, dribbling, shooting, schooling defenders, and winning ball games with less than a second left on the clock. He played in the rain, the blistering heat and the frigid cold. He played until he could barely walk home at night. He played late so he wouldn't have to go home to an empty house and sit alone.

As he grew tall, his desire for a father waned. He resented himself for holding on to a dream that could never come true. His hurt spawned an anger that birthed pride. In time he felt that his strength would not come from a familial foundation, but from the fame gained by his talent.

He looked at Preach through the small window. "You taught me I wasn't alone; that there was someone willing to give their life so I could live. Gator could have killed me. But you took his knife in my place."

Preah gazed at DeAndre long and hard. "The whole time that I've been in prison, I wasn't praying to share in your success. I saw you on TV. I watched you grow up by the praise of sports reporters and game announcers. If you played well, they loved you. If you missed a shot, they crucified you. I prayed that I could be the balance in your life. That's it.

"I can't give you all of those lost years back, and I wanted to do something for you for my son. I could never have predicted that you would end up here, or why. I didn't want that. But God had his plan, and it played out exactly as it was supposed to."

DeAndre could only smile at Preaches words. Somewhere in the recess of his inner psyche, the hurt little boy that he once was smiled too.

Preah pressed his fist to the glass. DeAndre did the same. "I'm glad that we got to spend that time together, DeAndre. That last year was the highlight of my life."

DeAndre wiped his tears. "How's Percy?"

"Cantankerous. Angry. Old. And a terrible loser."

DeAndre's laughter filled the small concrete space. "Sounds like he's doing just fine. Hasn't changed a bit."

Preach laughed too. "What about you? Don't be so quick to change the subject. I heard a little something-something on ESPN Radio last night."

"You heard something, huh?

"Well you know, I don't subscribe to rumors. I figured I'd go straight to the horse's mouth."

"It was supposed to be a surprise."

"There aren't any surprises when you're famous. I thought you knew that."

"I guess you're right. I signed a contract with the Toronto Raptors. It's the minors, but I'm playing. We finished training camp last week."

Preach clapped his hands and rubbed them together. "That's what I'm talking about. The road to redemption begins with the first step."

DeAndre held up a flat palm to stop him. "I'm in the D-league, Pop. We're talking peanuts a year."

"So what? It's exposure. We watch D-league games all the time. And it's a paycheck, isn't it? This time last year you were dribbling a basketball for free. Don't get all snooty now. You've got to start somewhere. You could be playing in Russia or the Ukraine, where nobody would see you."

DeAndre was still skeptical. "It could be a long time before I'm bumped up. If I'm bumped up to the NBA. I'm not as good as I used to be."

"You'll get it back, DeAndre. Trust in God. He didn't deliver you from this dungeon for nothing. He spared your life because you are destined for greatness. It has nothing to do with how good you are now or were back then, If your purpose is to shine paying basketball, then that's what you will do. But you'll never know if you keep thinking negatively. My God is an awesome God, son. He can do all things. Trust in Him, and He will guide you."

Faith had never been DeAndre's strong point, but he had to admit that he hadn't come this far on his own. He had ended up in prison, but the exact prison where his father was serving time. That couldn't have been by chance.

"I'll try," he told Preach. "And um there's something else that they didn't report on ESPN Radio."

Preach raised an eyebrow, "What's that?"

"Melody and I are getting married."

CHAPTER
TWENTY-ONE

Percy walked out of his cell carrying a blue plastic chair. He put it down beside Preaches, at a good distance from the TV. He sat down and looked around. Almost the entire cell block had their chairs out there and were chattering while waiting for the game to begin.

Percy asked, "What time does it start?"

Preach wouldn't take his eyes from the screen. "They're supposed to do a short documentary on Andre after the commercial break."

Percy's lip curled into what some would consider a smile, others a scowl. "I ain't never seen you so happy about anything."

"I don't know about happy," Preach told him. "Proud, maybe. A little nervous too."

The game announcers came back after the commercial.

"All right, Percy. The show is starting. Shut your big mouth."

"What you say?"

"I said shut your mouth. I want to watch my boy on TV."

"You keep on and I'm gonna run one across your eye and you won't be watching nothing. Telling me to shut up. My name is Percy P. Pendergrass."

The other inmates turned to Percy and shushed him just as the announcer introduced the biopic about DeAndre entitled, "Innocence Chained."

The screen went black. The ping of a bouncing basketball reverberated in a steady cadence. DeAndre spoke over the sound. "I never wanted to do anything else. Never saw myself doing anything else. I was born to ball."

The scene blinked to life, depicting a sixteen-year-old DeAndre dribbling alone on a blacktop basketball court. He was scrawny and awkward, but his eyes remained forward, focused n an unseen goal that lay ahead.

"DeAndre Harris," droned the narrator. "Born superstar, dominated basketball courts before anyone even knew him."

Vernon Jackson, a high school basketball coach, leaned back in his beaten leather chair in his office at Enloe High School. A wall of trophies gleamed behind him, in the center was a life-sized poster of DeAndre in his NC State Jersey. "I'd been coaching for thirteen years and had never thought we would make it very far. DeAndre came along and changed all that. I knew he would be great the first ten minutes of practice. I put him on our varsity team as a freshman. I'd never coached a player that was so talented. He was so good that I didn't know how to coach him. He broke the national high school scoring record halfway through the season. He took us to the state championship every year he was here, and we haven't been to one since he left."

In the next scene, DeAndre was going one-on-one with an opponent in a high school championship game. He threaded the ball through his legs, looped it around his back, then spun around his opponent as the boy tripped over his own feet and DeAndre leapt for a dunk.

Then he was sitting on a picnic table at a park, clean shaved and young, holding the basketball as if it were another appendage connected to his body.

An anonymous voice offscreen asked him, "Did you ever think that you would be coveted by so many colleges?"

He smiled shyly. "Maybe five or six. Not forty-nine."

"In the end," the Narrator continued as footage of DeAndre sitting at a table with fifty college sports hats, flashed on the screen. "DeAndre chose NC State." DeAndre shook hands with a NC State representative and slid on a black hat with WOLFPACK emblazoned above the bill.

"Harris decimated NCAA teams," the narrator declared as a montage of clips showing DeAndre dunking on various college teams rolled on with Waka Flocka's 'I Go Hard In The Paint' booming in the background. "Harris opted out of the one-and-done trend, popular with today's superstar youth, and let NC State to four consecutive national titles. NBA teams were hovering outside his door, salivating for the chance to snatch him up after graduation. And then tragedy struck."

The scenes of DeAndre's past triumphs and bright future were replaced with a dark street lit only by the flashing lights of police cars peppered across the front lawn of a frat house. Dozens of college students stood behind yellow CAUTION tape as a stretcher was wheeled out with a body bag on it.

Tabitha Murray, Harris' girlfriend, was gunned down during a fight at a frat party. Months later, DeAndre Harris was convicted of her murder.

DeAndre sat behind an oak table in the full courtroom during his trial.

Judge Regal Walters banged his gavel. "I'm sorry Mr. Harris, but I have no choice except to sentence you to life without the possibility of parole."

A still shot of Central Prison came into view. "Many believed that life was over for DeAndre Harris. Sentenced to life. Destined to die in prison. Who would have thought he would fight harder than he ever had on the basketball court and emerge innocent?"

Percy frowned to Preach. "Man, they didn't mention you at all."

Preach held up his hand. "It doesn't matter."

The footage cut to DeAndre who was on the sidelines, stretching for the night's game against the Portland Trail Blazers. Every man in the cellblock applauded.

The game announcer declared, "DeAndre Harris makes his debut in the NBA's Developmental League, so we will see if he's still got it. Tip off when we come back."

Percy turned to Preach when a commercial came on. "I don't understand why they don't start him. He's the best player out there."

"He's on the court. That's the important thing. He could be sitting here listening to you chew my head off with your nonsense."

Percy smacked his lips. "I'm tired of hearing you disrespecting me."

"Stop up your ears. Now shut up. The game is starting."

***

Coach Van Jenkins walked over to DeAndre on the bench. "How are you holding up?"

DeAndre smiled. "Phenomenal."

"Most guys in your position would be itching to start. How can you be so calm?"

"I'm just happy to be here, Coach. Many people don't realize how much of a blessing an opportunity like this is. I do."

Coach Jenkins laid a hand on DeAndre's shoulder. "I'll try to get you some playing time. Even if it's only for a few minutes."

After the coach had left, DeAndre sat quietly for a long while. This was the first time that he had ridden the bench in his life, but strangely he was at peace with it. He heard Preaches words echoing in his head, 'This time last year you were dribbling a basketball for free.' How could he not appreciate this course of his life? He eased back in his chair, knowing that he would be okay, even if he didn't get a chance to play.

He looked up in the stands and saw Melody sitting next to his mom. They waved, and so did he. Their joy was another sign that everything would work out.

***

"What are they doing?" Percy screamed at the TV. "Why don't they put DeAndre in the game? They're getting killed."

He was right. The Trailblazers dominated the first half of the game. It looked like a junior high school team was struggling against The Harlem Globetrotters.

Preach wouldn't be discouraged. "There's a reason they call it the D-League, Percy. They aren't the best players. Not yet."

A Trailblazer popped a three, and collective boos of disappointment echoed throughout the cellblock.

"Put DeAndre in the game!" One con yelled.

Percy turned to Preach. "I don't understand how you can be so calm. Don't you care?"

Preach remained still. "I do, but I won't get riled up over something I can't control. My faith is in God's hands. That's it. "

***

It happened at the top of the third quarter. Jabari Thompson, point guard for the Raptors, went up for a jump shot and landed with his ankle rolled on its side. He lay sprawled out on the hardwood floor for fifteen minutes while trainers poked and prodded, then determined that he need to go to the hospital.

Coach Jenkins hurried over to DeAndre as soon as Thompson was carried off the court. "Harris, you're up. We're down seventeen. I hate to put you in under so much pressure, but I don't have a choice."

DeAndre stood and yanked off his warm-ups." I'll do what I can."

***

"Look, y'all!" Percy pointed at the TV screen. "They put DeAndre in the game."

The whole block applauded and stomped their feet as DeAndre trotted onto the court. Preach just sat back with his arms folded over his chest and his eyes on the screen.

"Yes, sir!" Percy declared. "We 'bout to hand it to them now!"

***

Chauncy Taylor, shooting guard for the Raptors, inbounded the ball to DeAndre. As soon as it hit his hands, all of the nervousness and butterflies in his belly were gone. It was just him and the ball. Defenders approached in slow motion. One met him at half court, sinking low with his arms wide. DeAndre faked left. When the guy went with him, DeAndre grabbed his right wrist just enough to jerk him off balance while he reversed and took off in the opposite direction.

He weaved through Trailblazers like a sports car slaloming around orange road cones. He hopped and dropped an easy layup for his first two points of the game.

The crowd's celebration made the walls tremble.

A Trailblazer inbounded the ball. DeAndre ran over to cut it off. He snatched the ball mid-pass and launched into a 360-degree dunk that brought the crowd to their feet again.

The Trailblazers made it down to their side of the court on their next possession. The Raptors rebounded after a missed three-pointer. DeAndre wound up with the ball and gave his team time to set up. They fell under his leadership naturally. Defense was tight. A second defender ran over to trap DeAndre, but he passed the ball off, then sprinted for the goal. Chaunery Taylor lobbed the ball from deep. DeAndre leapt, caught the ball, and slammed it through the hoop.

His teammates trotted up the court with him. DeAndre accepted their praise, even though praise wasn't what he sought. He wanted to win.

The roaring crowd disappeared. All he heard was the sound of his own breath moving in and out in a smooth rhythm. This was the high he'd been chasing his entire life. Preach had been right the entire time. He was destined for greatness. Nothing could stop it. No Michael. Not Prison. Not Gator. Some things were meant to be, no matter what.

***

The stands emptied out and flooded the floor after the game. Hundreds shouted; "Har-ris!" "Har-ris!" "Har-ris!" Over and over again.

DeAndre stood smiling in the midst of it all. Reporters pushed through the crowd to get next to him.

"DeAndre," a female reporter began, "You single-handedly let your team to a thirty-point unanswered run to take the lead and coast through the fourth quarter. Is it safe to say that the phenom is back?"

"I, um…"

DeAndre's words were cut off by the sensation of someone wrapping their arms around him. It was Sonny Abrams, General Manager of the Raptors. "You did great tonight, DeAndre, really great."

The female reporter turned to Sonny. "Mr. Abrams, what do you see in the near future for DeAndre Harris? Do you think he performed well enough to silence he critics who said he'd lost his prime while a wrongfully convicted inmate?"

"Well," Sonny clapped DeAndre on the back. "He won't be in the D-league for long. I can tell you that. I'll ask him to finish out the summer season so he can get his legs back, but it's obvious that he's ready for us to take him to the next level. I've got a contact on my desk waiting for him to look over tomorrow." He leaned in close to the microphone. "And for any team thinking of making an offer, my contract well exceeds any four-year, four-million-dollar rookie deal. We're going all the way with DeAndre."

"Wow," she said. "DeAndre, what are your immediate plans?

The smile faded from his lips. "The first thing that I'm going to do is hire a legal team to get my father out of prison."

***

The cellblock came alive with inmates whooping and kicking cell doors. Many crowded around Preach to put him on the back.

Nothing could have ruined that moment... until Preach looked up and saw an officer leading Gator into the block with his property bags.

"What's all the hoopla for?" Gator asked, smiling. His eyes locked on Preach. "The party hasn't even started yet."

TWENTY-TWO

Preach refused to walk around the prison in fear. He did not trust Gator to let bygones be bygones, but he was not afraid of him either. If anything, he respected "Gator's power among the youth in the prison population. Keyvon and his other cronies were gone, yet it didn't take long for another group to fall in step behind him. It was the natural food chain of prison life, and Gator sat on his throne at the top. As long as he found a way to provide for his underlings, they would be willing to kill for him.

Percy offered him a shank. It was a shard of plexiglass with a serrated edge and tape-wrapped handle. "I've been hearing talk," he told Preah. "It's never been this bad. You need a little something to protect yourself."

He refused to take it. He hadn't been carrying one. Grace would be his protection. He awoke each morning reciting Psalm 23: "Yea though I walk through the valley of the shadow of death, I will fear no evil; for thou are with me; thy rod and thy staff they comfort me."

With faith in his heart, Preach did not feel invincible, but safe. He had never felt that he was walking alone. The Lord was always with him. Even when Gator's minions met him as he and Percy were walking the stairwell. Neither Preach nor Percy saw the three men standing on the landing above them until they were upon them. If Preach had been alone, he would have charged into the men in an attempt to catch them off guard. Since Percy was there, he turned and headed back downstairs. Three more ascended to the landing below them. They were boxed in.

"Y'all got beef with me," Preach told them. "Let Percy leave."

Percy dipped his hand in his pocket and slid out his knife. "I ain't going nowhere."

Preach softly whispered, "Lord, thank you for allowing me to spend time with my son. Protect him, Lord, for he is your own."

***

Terrell Wright struggled against two Lakers who had him trapped at the three-point line. DeAndre hustled to Wright's left and set a pick so he could roll away. Wright found an open lane, ran through it, then popped a shot. The ball hit the back of the rim and bounced out. James Taylor rebounded and passed the ball around as the Raptors tried in vain to get another open shot.

DeAndre glanced at the clock. Five seconds left in the fourth quarter, and they were down by one.

Wright got the ball back and drove straight into the paint, drawing three Lakers trying to foul him. His move left DeAndre wide open at the top of the key behind the three-point line. Wright slung the ball back to DeAndre with less than two seconds left.

Time stood still in DeAndre's mind. A camera's flashbulb exploded and paused while illuminated, looking like the north star beaming in the middle of the arena. Fans froze mid-clap. The whole place went silent as his gaze locked on the hoop and his hands launched the ball toward it.

The buzzer sounded as soon as it left his fingertips.

Swish.

Game time.

The end of the game was typical. Reports swarmed. Two months into the NBA's regular season and the usual motions were already old. The whole time that he stood sweaty and exhausted with a microphone thrust in his face, he really wanted to go to the locker room and shower.

It took thirty minutes for the interviews to end. In the locker room he noticed a stream of text messages from Melody. CALL ME NOW!

"Babe," he said as soon as she picked up the phone. "What's the emergency?"

"I hate to be the one that has to tell you this, but.. it's Preach."

"Preach? What happened?"

***

He caught the first flight out and made it to Wake Medical in Raleigh five hours after he stepped off the basketball court.

Sergeant Howell and Officer Leach were the prison guards charged with monitoring Preach during his hospital stay. They stood outside room 227. Both greeted DeAndre as he walked up.

"How are you, son?" Leach asked, shaking his hand.

"What's going on with my dad?"

"Gator sent his goons after him." The tone of Leach's voice was a somber one. "He was stabbed up pretty bad."

"Is he going to make it?"

Leach exhaled and looked away for a moment. "He's in bad shape, DeAndre."

"Can I see him?"

Sergeant Howell nodded. "I called Warden Branker personally. You've got thirty minutes."

Leach led him into the room. Preaches entire upper body was wrapped in blood-soaked bandages. Leach whispered that he'd been stabbed thirty-six times. The flowing blood stains made it look so much worse.

A nurse was just finishing checking his vital signs when they entered. As she exited, she told DeAndre, "He's been given a heavy dosage of morphine for the pain If he wakes, he'll drift in and out when you try to talk to him."

She left. Leach leaned against a far wall as DeAndre pulled up a chair next to Preaches bed.

DeAndre stared deep into Preaches closed eyes. "I feel like this whole thing is my fault. If it hadn't been for me, you never would have crossed paths with Gator. Or if I had stood up to Gator before you got involved..."

Tears seeped from DeAndre's eyes, but it was okay. He'd been holding them back for so long. With each drop, a little more of his pain washed away.

"I heard from Richard Steinberg. He told me that your commutation went through. He said that your sentence should be commuted to twenty years in sixty days." Preach showed no indication that he had even heard him. DeAndre reached out and squeezed his hand. "Did you hear me, Pop? You're going to be a free man again. All you have to do is get up and walk out of here. Just hold on a little longer. That's all you have to do. Please, Pop. Please. Don't die on me."

The EKG flatlined casting an echoing shriek through-out the room.

"What's going on?" DeAndre asked as six nurses and a doctor hurried into the room.

"Pop!" DeAndre screamed. "Pop!"

Leach and Sergeant Howell snatched DeAndre by the arms and dragged him out into the hallway. He spotted a nurse climb onto Preaches chest and start CPR as the door slowly closed in his face.

Leach wrapped him up in a hug as DeAndre cried on his shoulder. "Pray for him," Leach said. "That's all you can do now, DeAndre. Pray for his life and his soul."

Father God. I know my Dad hasn't been perfect, but if you never hear another of my prayers, please hear this one…

TWENTY-THREE

It was an unusually warm March day when DeAndre parked in the cemetery. He sat in his car for fifteen minutes, but Melody was nowhere to be seen. He got out and started up a steep hill toward a blue canopy with a mound of dirt beneath it. The casket had been lowered into the empty grave by the time he made it there.

Seeing the mahogany box at the bottom of the hole sent a cascading sadness through him. He knelt at the edge, thinking that no man should have to die the way he did, so savagely. Especially not someone dear to him. And for what? The pride and audacity of prison gangbangers. Senseless.

Soft teardrops splattered like rain on the surface of the casket.

So much stupidity surrounded his death. It took an act of congress to buy his body from the state. Five-hundred dollars. They had not wanted to release the man, even in death. And then the funeral home had been emptied during the wake. He'd been locked up so long that he didn't have family left to mourn him. Officer Leach was the only employee from the prison that showed up. He brought his wife. It was a nice gesture.

DeAndre stood and stared down into the earth and wondered how many would show up at his funeral. Then again, he wouldn't care if nobody came. It wouldn't matter at this point. He'd be dead. Yet still he whispered, "Lord, protect him."

He turned and saw Melody struggling to push Preach up the hill in his wheelchair. DeAndre trotted down the hill to help her.

"I could have done it by myself." She said when he took the handles from her.

"I know, "he said, smiling. "But I got it. You're too pretty to work hard. Take a break."

After they made it up the hill, Preach pulled himself up by holding onto DeAndre's shoulder. It was a struggle to stay on his feet, but he was determined to stand tall.

"Percy," Preach said while looking down at the casket. "You were the most vile, hateful, and meanest creature I ever knew. But while on this earth, I found no better friend. If it hadn't been for you, I would be a dead man. There are no words that can thank you enough."

Melody reached out and wiped the warm tears streaming down his cheeks.

Preach reached into his pocket and pulled out a single chess piece. A black King. "I wish you could be out here with me. Lord knows that you deserved to be. We got used to the confined space of the inside. The first thing that amazed me was how big the world seemed to be, yet so empty without you in it." Preach dropped the black King into the grave. "You won, Percy. You won."

DeAndre grabbed his father and held him when he broke down. He hated that Percy had been killed, but he admired the sacrifice.

Percy kept three of the gangbangers at bay during the attack in the stairwell. He killed no one, but he held them off long enough for officers to arrive and break it up. He died on the way to the hospital.

All six gang members were charged with his murder, and Gator was charged with conspiracy, because he sent out the order. He would receive another life sentence for his role.

As much as DeAndre thought Gator was given a fitting punishment, he was burdened by the fact that Percy had to die in the process.

DeAndre helped Preach down to his wheelchair. "Come on, Pop. We've got somewhere to be."

***

They arrived at the Apex High School gym an hour later, twenty minutes late. The kids were already inside. He and Preach traveled beneath a huge banner that hung over the closed doors of the gym which read: "Welcome to The DeAndre Harris Mini Camp for Kids!"

Fifty kids ranging in age from twelve to fifteen, were spread across the floor working with a large group of basketball coaches and players who had volunteered their time to be there. DeAndre had chosen the 'age range' to help inner-city kids who were most at risk of joining gangs and ending up in prison.

He hated Gator for the man he was, but DeAndre felt that Gator could have turned out to be a different man if given the right opportunities. So, when he looked out among that group of teens, he hoped that he could save them all, and in that way, spare a life in the future.

"Hey everybody! Gather around!" One of the camp coaches hollered. "We've got a special guest that wants to meet you."

All fifty kids ran over and surrounded DeAndre. The smiles on their faces were enough to make him feel like the happiest man alive.

"Many of you know that I went to prison for a crime I didn't commit," he began. "And as much as I hate to admit it, many of you will end up there., for crimes you will commit, if you make bad choices. That is a reality. But I set up this camp to give you a better goal to reach for. We can't all be basketball players. I'm good with a ball, but I can't draw or paint well. You each have an individual talent that defines you, and even though we'll be having fun, we'll also be working to find programs that interest you close to your home. Our intention is to show you that there is much more to life than the streets, and if you work hard, you can do anything you want to in this world. Now, I won't always be here. I'll be traveling and playing games, but in my absence, I leave you with a man that I aspire to be like every day. My dad, Preach Harris."

The kids clapped. Preach rolled to the forefront in his wheelchair. "Before I tell you about prison, and why you should do all you can to avoid it, let me first introduce you to my father my heavenly father for all things are possible when you trust in him. Please bow your heads. Father God...

SureShot Books
PUBLISHING LLC
Books have the POWER
to change lives!